Buddy Why

Steven Salmon

AmErica House
Baltimore

Copyright © 2000 by Steven Salmon

All rights reserved. No part of this book may be reproduced in any form without written permission from the publishers, except by a reviewer who may quote brief passages in a review to be printed in a newspaper or magazine.

First printing

ISBN: 1-58851-828-0
PUBLISHED BY
AMERICA HOUSE BOOK PUBLISHERS
www.publishamerica.com
Baltimore

Printed in the United States of America

I dedicate the book to the memory of my father, Donald Wallis Salmon. I will always love him, and cherish the short time we had together on Spruce Knoll.

I want to thank my mom, Mary Salmon, for her never ending love and support through all of my life. Without her sacrifice I wouldn't have reached my potential or dreams. I owe everything in my life to her. I want to thank Larry Watson, my writing mentor who made me believe that I had talent to be a writer. I want to thank my best friend, Amber Tilley for editing the novel, and for always being a friend. To my sister, Susan, I will always love you. Thank you for being a great sister. I want to thank the following people. David Strong, Jessie Andersen, Christine Fredricks, Richard Behm, Donna Decker, Ruth Dorgan, Stephen Odden, Joan Collins, Patrick Barlow, William Colby, Franklin Cham, Josh Tilley, Jon Bain and all of my relatives for supporting me.

Chapter One

The Massy Ferguson 44O purred along the thicket of clover and wild grasses as the rusty bush hog spewed out the clippings from behind the wheels of the mower. A boy with a stream of drool flowing from his lips was cradled on the right knee of his father who had wrapped an arm around the chest of his son-me. I pretended to be a farmer cutting hay as I mouthed "Varoom, varoom," while seeds of milkweed and grass flew across the meadow. This was my fond memory of Daddy and me being together working on the farm. Wherever Daddy was, I was usually close by. I wanted to experience every task he did. Rays of sunshine cast down upon the tractor as steam rose from the Massey into the blue sky. Now and then a cluster of elms offered a cool respite from the glaring heat. Daddy steering, shouted, "Duck!" when a branch came to our height. I bent my head as Daddy did. *Crash*, *boom*, *pop* rumbled and echoed from the hog as shreds of a torn limb, which had fallen in a thunderstorm, appeared, mangled from the sharp blades.

I thought fireworks were being set as my body jumped, but I knew what had happened in my mind. "Hey Buddy, don't jump like that," as drool drizzled down on the hairy bronzed forearm of the man. The two of us rounded the corner of the prairie where a gleaming object was stationed next to a pile of seasoning maple and oak firewood. "Let's take a break and eat lunch," he whispered into my ear. Only this time I didn't leap as Dad nibbled on my earlobe.

"Okay, Daddy. I hungry." I heard a loud clattering noise as the rotation of the blades whirled about, kicking up dust. Daddy proceeded to the stack of wood where he halted the red machine. The moment he turned off the mower and took the key from the ignition, all became a peaceful silence. I looked over the half-cut field, admiring our morning's work. Daddy swung his left leg over the steering wheel and put both of his hands under me. He stepped down and away from the Massey, carrying me like a sack of grain over to my wheelchair. The scent of newly mown grass tickled our nostrils. He placed me in my chair. I hollered, "Ouch!" The heat retained by the black vinyl of the seat burned my skin.

"Sorry about that, Trey. I forgot to cover it with a towel. I should've known better, godammit."

"I okay, Buddy. No big deal. Okay, what we do now?" Both of us sometimes refered to each other by the nickname of Buddy. I usually called him Daddy.

"Well, we've got to grease the joints of the mower before we cut again." I sighed because I wanted to cut more of the tall grass waving at me. Daddy went over to the tractor and opened a tool box that had a grease gun. He held the barrel in one hand and returned to me where he would be working. I always had to see everything Daddy did. He popped a wheely to push me through the dense thicket as the front tires wobbled around in the air. I imagined myself in a Bobcat working on a pile of earth, breaking it up by slamming my bucket into the soil. The grease gun flopped on the left side of Daddy almost like a worm oozing out from him. I giggled with glee, enjoying the bouncy ride over to the hog. Daddy said, "I have a surprise for you." He parked me by the mower and pulled out a couple of peanut butter and cheese crackers from his shirt pocket. He yanked the wrapper off and popped one into my mouth and the other into his.

I grinned as peanut butter stuck to the roof of my mouth while bits and crumbs of orange fell all over me. Daddy removed clumps of grass from the belts of the mower to begin greasing. He glanced at me and knew I was bored. "I also have a PayDay here, but you'll have to wait until I'm finished."

He picked up the gun to caulk the joints. "Why do grease? Boring, Daddy."

"I know it is, Buddy. But it helps the belts, which propel the blades to run smoothly. Just as the tractor needs gas, oil and water to go. Everything is connected in some fashion." A rabbit leaped out of the tall grass to snatch up a couple sprigs of clover. I gazed at the bunny's whiskers bobbing up and down as it munched away at a tender stalk of grass.

"I see. Like that rabbit over there."

He looked up to where my eyes were pointing and was pleased with my observation. "Exactly, son. Well. I'm just about through and we can roll again. Of course, after we eat the candy bar." I was grinning from ear to ear. I was always happy to make Daddy proud of me and to be with him. The cottontail hopscotched back into the green jungle with its meal in tow. Daddy returned the grease gun to the tool compartment and ran his blackened hands on the ground. He then pulled out a thin white package from his denim jeans. "Why don't we sit in the shade to get out from the glare?" I nodded my reddened face with beads of perspiration running down my forehead.

Daddy thrust up the front of the wheelchair, heading for a white barn nearby. My head rocked back and forth, knocking between the handlebars and making me feel like a pendulum in a clock. I was always afraid of the darkness of the barn because of the spooky rattles and beating wings of bats flying out of the loft. "Ah, this is better, Buddy."

"Yeah, Daddy." My wheelchair left tracks in the finely compacted mix of dirt and cow manure with tufts of straw laying on top of the rich soil. Mildew and cobwebs had taken over the place. *No Smoking* signs were posted on doors and walls to warn people against lighting up. A sheet metal shed was attached to the barn along with a dairy parlor that had been blocked off. I always wanted to coast down the cement ramp with a rusty railing where cows had trod up to be milked, and Daddy would catch me at the bottom. But we were beat as we strolled past a hay trough filled with an assortment of metal objects, lumber, rolls of fencing wire, a drawer, loose hay and a scoop shovel. Dung around the feeder had formed into an image of a burial mound. Pine tar from the poles of the tin shack filled the air as a light breeze shook the metal exterior of the feeding area.

Daddy drew me to the abandoned hay loft, opening up into the old white barn. He lifted me over a three foot embankment to a wooden platform covered with dust, and wheeled me to a stack of two-by-fours. After he sat down on the boards, we ate the caramel-nougat bar in solitude. I was gazing at the eerie but neat features that appeared to me to be in working condition. To the right of me, sun filtered through the siding, decayed from years of weathering. Missing slats gave a view of bare soil curved in a *C* around the barn. Groundhogs lived under the floor and at dawn each day would pop out to chew away on the tender green soy bean plants, leaving naked stems poking to the blue sky. In front of me was a massive floor strewn with straw, and I felt like an actor performing on stage because of the high openness of the platform. The length was about twenty yards and was about forty yards wide. On the other side of where we sat was a sudden drop-off that I imagined to be an orchestra pit. But it was just a shack for storing Daddy's implements and had been discarded by the dairy farmer. I peered in the hollow hole and saw a trailer, a three-bottom Harrison plow, a rusty disk, a Farmall attachable frontloader with monster, fang-like teeth, a blade for grading gravel or snow. Lying against the wall was a giant steel loop from a defunct silo, which to me looked like an onion ring.

In the center of the barn rose two parallel square beams supporting the rafters and connecting a second level of beams with wooden pegs. I was always amazed how the wooden infrastructure fit together without a single nail, almost like being held by an invisible hand. Behind me was a half-open stable door with no horse's head to pet or give sugar. Inside hung a broken bridle and saddle for riding. Leaning against the door was a pitchfork. I was eyeing a ladder on the wall as I swallowed my last bite. "Where that go?"

Daddy saw the direction of my eyes as he rested his head on the boards of the stall.

"Oh, the ladder goes to a second landing." We had eaten all of our junk food, and Daddy took off his glasses to wipe away smudges of grime with his T-shirt. He had a belt buckle with the gold letters *SAM* that gleamed in the darkness. After readjusting his bifocals he saw my questioning eyes pointing upwards.

"What that up?"

He stood up beside me to see what I was focused on. "You mean that circular piece of metal hanging from the top?" He could barely see the device from where he was standing with his poor sight.

"Yeah, Daddy."

"A pulley system rigged up to bring bales up to the second story, which I told you about already."

"Why?" I muttered as a bubble burst from my mouth and with bits of nuts still clinging to my teeth.

"Because it was easier to move heavy objects around. My Buddy is always asking questions. You need to know lots of information since you are the son of an engineer. Well, are you ready to mow again? Always remember to finish what you started."

"Okay, RaRa now, Daddy." He laughed at my expression for the tractor as he grasped the handlebars to push me to the meadow. I giggled as Daddy made diesel engine noises as we chugged along. "Buddy, I love you," I said.

"I love you, too." He stopped the wheelchair to embrace me, and I gave him a wet kiss on his stubbled cheek. For a moment we were one. Once separated, he unfastened my seat belt and tossed me up on his broad shoulders. My legs hung down onto his chest with his right arm held snugly across my bony kneecaps to keep me in an upright position. Being up high I felt as though I was riding a camel with my head swaying in motion. I was unaccustomed to having such a high view. It made me feel that I could reach the horizon with my fingertips. Being in a wheelchair always meant looking up at everything and everyone around me. Daddy's steady and even gait marched toward the Massey. I turned back and saw the whole barn shrink before me with each step Daddy took.

He climbed aboard the red hunk of metal with me still soaking up the heights and green foliage from distant fields. I always thought of myself as a country boy. I loved how in the spring the rebirth of green was all around us with new crops growing and grass thickening. But in the fall, leaves fell from the trees and the fields turned brown at harvest time. I would lie in bed at night listening to the distant hum of tractors planting or bringing in the grain from the fields until I fell asleep. I learned life went in cycles, and I was a part of the evolution of the farming community. He sat down and jostled me from his shoulders to his lap. I let out a sigh of disappointment because I wasn't part of the atmosphere anymore. "Are you comfy?"

"Yeah."

He smiled as he placed his arm around me. With a flick of the wrist, he turned the key in the ignition and pressed the starter button several times with his thumb. A black ball of smoke belched out the back, trailed by a series of black rings showing against the brilliant sky. The tires began to rotate slowly until he kicked it into third. I was excited when the RaRa suddenly leapt forward across the freshly cut furrows to the beckoning triangle of wild tall grass. The bushhog jingled from behind as Daddy drove to the base of the triangle. He raced the Massey into the bowing weeds and came to an abrupt halt. I heard a loud rumble as a tug was given to a wire on the left-rear tire rim to fire up the mower. The blades were striking nothing but air. Daddy shifted to the creeping second gear which I hated because it wasn't fast enough for me. The clattering became a shishing hum as fragments of clover and grass danced about in the air.

Time passed by. Dusk approached from the west, tints of red and blue jutting into the creamy, yellowish sky. "One more lick and we'll have it, Bud," Daddy shouted to me as he made a circle in the middle of the pasture. I was happy to watch a small parcel of hay still standing, but in an instant it was squashed and shredded by the rusty hog. He ripped the wire to the mower with three quick pulls to shut off the whining belts. A hush came over us with only the engine purring. Daddy paused to admire our work like a barber checking to see if he had cut every strand of hair. He gazed up at the colorful, picturesque heaven above. "Oh, Buddy, it's going to be a beautiful day tomorrow."

"How you know?" I was amazed how he knew by just looking up at the clouds. The Massey gingerly strolled over to the gray metal pole shed.

"By the color of the sky. It's so pretty and red. Red sky at night, sailor's delight." The red machine hip-hopped to the feedlot, where my wheelchair sat under the tin roof.

"Oh, I see." The engine echoed off the metal box before Daddy killed the motor. Silence took over the scene, and the only sound was the dinging from the radiator. Hot water dripped over the front axle down to the ground. Daddy side stepped the steering wheel and cradled me with both arms as he stood up. He had begun to deliver me over to my chair when I said, "Potty can't wait." I was carried over to some burdock growing inside the shed door and he unzipped my fly. I leaned against his frame for support. Daddy fished out my penis from my underpants and held the private part pointed towards the weed.

"Go Buddy." A yellow stream rained on the thin broad green leaves to be absorbed into the soil. When the hissing ended, he asked, "Are you done?" I nodded to him as he put me back together. "Good aim, Trey; you hit the pole." We laughed at my marking on the post. I was held in his arms again to be transferred to my chariot. He carried me over to my wheelchair and strapped the seat belt around my stomach.

He tilted up the chair to head out of the hollow metal shack along a grassy slope. I was bounced around by the rough terrain and felt as though I was being thrashed about in a pickup crossing plowed furrows of a field. "How you know. If it's icky. Tomorrow?"

"Well, when the sky is red in the morning, sailors take warning as the old folk tale goes." Daddy huffed and puffed our way up a steep hill leading to the driveway. His face was beet-red and he appeared to be on the verge of collapsing. Sweat trickled down Daddy's forehead and clouded his bifocals, distorting his vision. A white brick, two-story farmhouse with battered olive shutters stood there. The wheelchair darted along the smooth stone surface, occasionally catching a pebble or two, delaying our progress to the front porch. He pushed me past a white wooden, two-story garage, where he stored his blue Ford 4x4, a Ford tractor with a belly mower for cutting the lawn, and a tan van. Paint was peeling off the building, falling into the surrounding rose bushes. Daddy reversed the wheelchair up to the cement steps of the porch and lifted me up. I thought I was a dolly being rolled to the blue front door. "RaRa pull tomorrow, Daddy."

"Yes, after I get back from work. We'll go to the fairgrounds, I promise." He swung open the door and we disappeared into the coolness of the house. I giggled as I thought about all the fun Daddy and I were going to have at the pull together as the door slammed closed.

Chapter Two

I sat on the porch listening to a set of wind chimes that dangled from the overhang and blew sweet music in my ears. "Hurry up, Ma. I walk now. Because Daddy comes," I demanded. Mom lugged a square metal contraption that had four wheels attached to a metal rectangle. A piece of cloth, striped like a train engineer's cap, was attached to a smaller rectangle on the top. The fabric had two holes for my legs to fit into. She placed the walker in the middle of the lane below the porch steps. (I always called my Mother, Ma, since it was easier for me to say.)

Mom transferred me from the wheelchair to the walker. She lifted me above the soft material and slowly brought my bony legs down through the flexible slots. Once I was in, Mom adjusted the inseam around my crotch, because I hated getting pinched in my private area. Before I could start on my race, Mom had to remove her stout belly, which was blocking my path. "Now remember not to go on the road and keep away from the ditch. You hear me? And move over to the side of the grass when you get to the end to let your father through. I'll be in the garden weeding."

"Yea, yea, Ma. Go go go, okay." She jumped out of the way. Mom watched me line up over one of the tire tracks packed firm by the constant pounding of trucks and heavy farm equipment. I wore red high-top Converse shoes, because the soft fabric could be tightened to my ankles, and other "in style" footwear would cut into me or would fall off. I shuffled onward as the wheels spurted now and then. I walked pigeon-toed toward my destination. The first fifty yards or so was wide open. The meadow was about twenty yards away on the right and overlooked the Fortson's red brick ranch house. Mike Fortson had owned the farm before we bought it. He was forced to retire due to a heart attack and could no longer do the strenuous physical labor anymore. I called him the mower man because he was always on his Cub Cadet, cutting his lawn in precise patterns like professional baseball diamonds. Every other day he was seen driving the Cub and wearing a scowl and an International hat on his head, rain or shine. I always felt sorry for his wife, Jean, because she had to trim and edge the property every time he mowed. He would instruct her on how to do something to his specifications or she would have to repeat the entire process over until he was satisfied. I was scared of him because he didn't smile.

To my left of me was an open expanse about the same size as the right side of the driveway. Beyond was the garden where Mom kneeled between the radishes and peas with a yellow bucket. Her head would pounce up and down, checking on me. I remember an evening she was weeding, and I was watching her, when a man got out of his Buick to dump an unwanted cat by the road. He was surprised when Mom sprung up and cursed at him, which made him rethink his plan. We had so many stray or sick animals left at our doorstep by city people. He took off, and Mom kept screaming like a witch, pointing her trowel at him.

A row of elms interspersed with rhubarb, gooseberries,

currents and horseradish stood next to a grassy lane by the soybean field. Mom canned all kinds of fruits to make delicious homemade jam. Also she stored vegetables from her garden patch for the winter in Mason jars in the basement. She would buy food we didn't grow ourselves, like cherries and apples, at the Rockton orchard.

    I was at the halfway point of my hike to meet Daddy. I took a break under the shade of three towering blue spruces to let the cool wind wipe away the sweat from my back and brow. One blue spruce was smaller than the pair on the left. The larger of the pair had a black stripe running down the middle of the godly giants. Every five feet was a steel knot from the base to about twenty feet because a tornado had split the tree almost in half. Daddy managed to nurse and mend the ugly sight by use of his bare hands and abundant knowledge.

    I always had to be with Daddy. I remember when he was remodeling the bathroom, ripping out old plaster or tearing down the rickety overhang above the porch. I would watch him hack at the rubble while he used a hammer or crow bar as chunks of debris fell everywhere. When he took a break, I would question why the roof had to be removed. Daddy told me it was rotten and had served its purpose, but the material was no longer stable. All things wear out sometimes, and he said he felt as if he too was about ready to give out at times. I laughed at his remark since I was too young to know Daddy was being serious. I always believed he had all the answers for life's problems.

    Once we had gone for a ride to Brooks, where he worked as a technical engineer. One late Sunday afternoon, we traveled the half hour trip to unload junk. Daddy backed into a dock where a red open dumpster sat. I felt we were doing something illegal since no one was around and all was quiet. I asked Daddy if it was all right for us to do this without anyone's knowledge. He stood outside the door, grimacing while he snapped a clump of plaster on his knee before tossing the two severed bits in the trash. His response was, "No one will ever care. It's just garbage, and will be gone in the morning before anyone gets here. Vip doesn't give a damn what I do. Just so long as I do what I'm told." He climbed onto the bed, and started to pitch pieces in the dumpster. I didn't understand what he was going through. Looking back now, I think Daddy was reaching out for help.

    I heard a train whistle blowing in the distance, which meant I had to keep going because Daddy would be arriving soon. I could see semi trailers riding piggyback and grain cars clinking down the tracks beyond the tasseling cornfield across the road. The railroad was a mile away, but I had excellent vision and was able to read the companies' names chugging by. I pursued onward. I had to be more alert now for the green balls from the walnuts scattered about the front lawn. I would navigate around nature's tennis balls because they would get stuck in my wheels and tip me over. I learned to punt them out of the way with my feet. Elms stood here and there, and I grinned to myself because I was almost at the end of the lane. I gave one more mighty stride forward before lurching onto the grass, away from the ditch and the culvert.

    I waited for Daddy to come and take me back to the

house in the truck. I would look at the white and salmon stones in the road, congealed in the oil like crackerjacks glued to peanuts. The corn was beginning to develop ears that I thought were listening to me talk about tractors. I was five yards away from two white posts attached to a stained maple wooden plank that read Spruce Knoll. On either side of the sign were two decaying stumps. Trees lost to Dutch Elms disease. Sometimes individuals would stop to drag me back to the house because they would be concerned that I was lost or neglected. I would scream, " Maaaaa!" Mom usually tried to wave off the do-gooder or shout, "He's okay," to the person. Once a man hauled me all the way to the house ranting and raving to Mom about abandoning her deformed drooling son by the pavement alone. I was furious because I had followed my parents' rules and was missing my chance to be in the pickup. Mom told the gentleman I was all right, but he walked down the driveway shaking his head. (I don't know why in some people's eyes I can't be by myself.) What boy doesn't love to roam on his own? All of the neighbors grew accustomed to our game and knew I needed the exercise for my legs. If I ventured onto the road or was too close to the ditch, they would instruct me to back up. I had to listen to them, because word about my actions always traveled back to Mom or Daddy. If I didn't obey, I would lose my privilege of meeting Daddy.

 All was quiet today. Wild daisies fluttered against the mailbox, where the name *Pike* was painted on the tin compartment screwed to a battered white pole. I glanced behind me at the green shingled roof of the house with a red brick chimney to the gradual slope of the grassy knoll to where the old barn sat. The landscape was teeming with green; fields of corn and beans were bountiful. Spruce Knoll was my farm. (I was raised here, and the beauty of the place still exists in my mind like an American lithograph. Years have passed, but when I hear the word *farm* mentioned, I always see Spruce Knoll, because I believe a piece of me never left.)

    I swung around because I heard the *putt-putt* of an old John Deere. It approached, pulling two hay wagons stacked with golden straw. I smiled at Cooter, my neighbor, waving to me as he whisked by. I always wondered why farmers would put three bales on the top, forming an Egyptian-shaped pyramid. I thought the bales would tumble off. Loose particles of straw flew about in the air, gently dropping like feathers to the ground. I was looking down when I heard the crunch of gravel beside me, startling me. Daddy drove in and sprang from the truck to fetch me, "Hi there, Buddy. Ready for some pulling tonight?"

    "Yea, yea, Daddy," I said in an excited tone as he lifted me into his arms. He carried me over to the passenger side and delivered me to an olive seat resting on the blue interior. Daddy had cut off a bar stool and placed it inside his pickup so I was able to see more easily. The seat gave me support because the curved sides enveloped my trunk. He buckled me in and closed the door, returning to the walker with what he had made for me. *Kerplunk*, echoed in the bed as Daddy threw in the apparatus and hopped into the cab. My eyes blinked when he slammed his door, because whenever I heard a loud noise, I would jump because of my startle reflex. The Ford barreled down the lane as I stared at Daddy. "How work?"

"All right I guess. Nothing you would be interested in. And yours?" I nodded affirmative to him. "How about if we get something to eat at the pull? Have a corn dog with a drumstick and homemade lemonade to wash it down."

"Yeaaaaaa, Daddy." We loved to eat junk food. Mom rarely kept anything sweet in the house except for pails of ice cream, which Daddy ate by the gallon. He always had two bowls after supper. He loved Butter Brickle and Butter Pecan. If he could, he would have eaten just ice cream. When I did something good, like receive an *A* on a test, I was rewarded with two scoops of chocolate by Daddy for a job well done.

"All right then, it's settled. We'll eat there." He patted my knee as the truck made a doughnut beside the garage and the house. I smiled when the pickup came to a grinding halt by the porch. "Let me say hello to Amber and your Ma. Then we'll be off. Do you have to go pee?"

"No, I okay." Daddy stepped out and switched the walker for the wheelchair. He then used a rubber tie down, which had hooks on both ends to secure the frame to the side of the pickup bed. Daddy took my walker inside after he made sure the chair was firmly connected to the driver's side. Before closing the front door, Daddy gave me the thumbs-up sign like the Fonz. I was becoming excited because I would have my Buddy the entire night without any Mom or Amber pestering us. Daddy was gone and my attention turned to a fire helmet shaped sticker on the back window behind me. The letters *S.R.F.D.* were printed in black across the emblem. A ladder was set against a burning flame with a hose splashing water on the red dancing ember. I was proud of Daddy being a volunteer fireman, because he was my hero. Once we came upon a blazing barn. Help was on its way, but too late to save the building filled with Harley Davidsons a man collected. I sat in the truck watching Daddy run a Ford tractor that had a plow behind it, which he used to create a fire break around the surrounding woods to contain the blaze to the barn. If he hadn't, more damage would have happened to neighboring property.

I was bored waiting. I leaned over to fumble around the knobs on the radio and gear shift. I grabbed the steering wheel with my long skinny hands and fingers. A CB dangled from the ceiling of the truck. Daddy loved radios and anything electronic. He was always playing with things that had dials or microphones. I pretended I was B. J. and the Bear in a big rig coasting along a highway. My back was tiring and I had to struggle to regain my balance in the seat and bring myself to an upright posture. I thought about the two hours it took me to walk the distance of the driveway, but I realized how short the lane was when riding in the pickup, which took about two minutes. It was still a huge physical challenge for me. I was daydreaming when Daddy opened the door and bolted into the cab. Daddy started up the engine as Mom and Amber, with her golden curls, waved at us. Mom mouthed, "Have a good time" to me. I nodded back and Daddy blew a kiss to his wife and daughter. He zoomed down the driveway, creating a cloud of dust behind.

Chapter Three

Daddy gunned his truck over country back roads amidst fields of green corn and soybeans. Mixed in the patchwork of growing green were segments of wheat turned gold or being harvested. Purple blooms of milkweed and the raspberry color of thistles blotted the yellowness. We passed a farmer combining his wheat. I watched the rotating beaters of the reaper chewing and shredding the stalks from the kernels. Straw spewed out the rear end of the red harvester onto the ground into neat rows to be raked and baled for bedding. I always saw work being done when I rode anywhere, because my eyes roved back and forth. I loved to view big farm machinery.

I had a game I played called "Guess What Type of Farm We Passed." I would look at the different buildings of operation. Large round steel bins connected to other bins by pipes meant the farmer grew cash crops: corn, soybeans and wheat. A long sheet-metal shack with fans on the exterior was either a pork or poultry producer. I could tell which by the smell of the manure. Concrete silos reaching to the blue horizon like city skyscrapers meant cattle for beef. I would see black and white or tan cows milling about in a pasture meaning a dairy must be near. Once in awhile, we passed a farm that had overgrown weeds and paint peeling off the surrounding sheds. If the house was boarded up without any signs of equipment around, it meant the owners had retired or sold out. I always was scared of these abandoned homesteads, because I thought ghosts or the devil lived there.

I remember once taking a ride with Daddy. He stopped the truck at a wayside near a meandering river. I didn't know why he had parked behind the old brick power plant next to the small park that had swings, a slide and two white outhouses. Daddy sat silently gazing at the rolling hills with oaks and maples while I stared at a suspension bridge that fishermen used. I felt strange because Daddy seemed lost in space, looking up at the heavenly blue sky. Suddenly he picked me up and carried me on his shoulders to the walkway. I was quiet, savoring the tranquil beauty of the countryside, but I was nervous when he stood in the middle of the bridge. I felt the wires swaying underneath, and thought I was going to fall or the bridge would snap in half. Daddy reassured me everything was all right and nothing bad would ever happen. I always believed I would be protected from harm with Daddy by my side. We went back to the pickup and headed for home. (Now I see the little warning signs that would end the comfortable life I knew.)

"We are almost there, Buddy." I gave out a yelp of joy as Daddy came to a screeching halt. Traffic was lined up for a quarter mile. Daddy leaned back in his seat. "It's always hurry up and wait, Buddy." I didn't know what he meant by that, but I begin to pout, my upper lip drooping over my famous happy face. " You'd better get used to it."

"Why?"

"Because that's how it is. At work I sit and wait for people to come to me with their problems on the assembly line. The minute someone arrives at my office, they expect an answer in an instant because they want everything

NOW." (I didn't know how true his statement was until I became older.) We inched our way forward toward a policeman waving a baton in his right hand, helping cars into the entrance of the Trenton County Fairground. He would blow his whistle to signal the vehicles to pull up and use his left hand to motion individuals to stop again.

"Why people keep others waiting, Daddy?"

"I wish I had an answer for that. But I don't. Where do you come up with these questions?" He went forward another fifty yards.

"I don't know." Daddy scratched his head and laughed. I peered to my right and saw a giant blue rattle that had the letters *SPRINGROCK* in bold colors encircling the head. On the left, the neon lights of the ferris wheel twinkled in the dusk, people's feet hanging out of the gondolas. We were almost to the gate when Daddy poked his head out of the driver's side window and shouted, "I'm fire personnel." The cop nodded to him to move over to the right by a trash barrel and some pylons.

The officer came over to us after he was relieved of his post by a man in an orange suit who looked like an escaped convict to me. "Sorry I didn't see you sooner." He stood against the driver's door. He tipped his gallon hat (which had a silver star badge in front) at us. I grinned at him.

"It's okay. How do I get to the grandstand from here?"

"Follow the blue, white and red flags around the outskirts of the midway and turn right on the hill by the pig barn. Go dead straight past Tilley's Implement Dealers display and you're there. Please drive slowly because people just don't pay attention to where they're going, especially the little ones. I'll radio Tiny you're coming, and he will meet you at the gate."

Daddy glanced at me to see if I heard the directions because he always was forgetting, but I always remembered everything. "Got that Buddy?"

"Yea."

Daddy's face shifted to the deputy, "Sounds good to me." He squinted his eyes because the sun reflected off the windshield.

"Be careful and have fun tonight with front row seats in the infield." We smirked at the cop, trudging back to being a human stop light. Both of us enjoyed the perks that came with being a volunteer fireman. Daddy went down the narrow service path following the flapping patriotic triangles tied to green metal stakes. The cab shook because of the bumps and ruts made by semis, golf carts and pumper trucks. Trailers ringed the inside of the fence, which made me frown, because managers of the amusement rides lived there. I loved to go on the bumper cars or the Tilt-o-Whirl, and Daddy carried me on his shoulders to get on the rides. He would go along with me, but sometimes an operator denied access because I was "crippled" and could get hurt. We needed the operator's supervisor's permission before I could go on many of the rides. Daddy would talk to the manager pointing to me in my wheelchair and explain about my handicap. There was a fifty-fifty chance of me being allowed a ride. I didn't understand why some persons made a fuss about my disability, but I gradually learned to accept this discrimination, because it would be a part of my life.

Cables snaked on the ground while the smell of

popcorn, cotton candy, caramel apples and french fries made me hungry. I saw people standing in line for rides and food and games. I heard vendors shouting, "Get a free toss to win a stuffed animal" or, "Try your luck to win a goldfish." The constant hum of generators hooked to refrigerated trucks sounded like a live hornets' nest to me. Music from a merry-go-round played in my mind, and I kept picturing cowboys chasing Indians in a circle because of the painted western murals on the carrousel.

Daddy swung onto the lane of crushed stone mixed with tar and oil which had an odor of rotten eggs. "Watch for people for me, Buddy." I nodded to him. Crisscrossing our path were mothers pushing baby carriages, love birds holding hands and kids running amuck from their parents. Both of us kept our eyes peeled for a person who might dart out from the barns or sparkling new farm equipment. The smell of sawdust, hay and straw combined with green animal droppings was a pleasant scent to my nose. I always had to laugh at adults and children dashing out of the livestock sheds holding their breath exclaiming, "Oh Yuck! Phew!" What was the big deal? I thought dung was a natural process of living. Wheelbarrows and pitchforks, ready to clear away manure, stood against the white poles of the barns. The pickup bounced over corncobs still oozing butter on the sticky black surface. I gazed at the trash barrels, brimming over with discarded paper, lining the way by Tilley's display. I wondered how individuals could create so much junk and not seem to care. Chopper boxes, balers, spreaders, hay rakes, mowers and a large harvester made people appear to be ants crawling about the equipment.

"Where RaRas?" The cement pillars of the grandstand came into view as the crowd filed into the dark recesses under the stands. Inside the bowels of the bleachers were the concessions and restrooms. I felt like a distinguished guest because I was right down where all the action would be taking place. There were more food vendors on the fringes selling brats, beer, nachos, hot dogs and hamburgers.

"All of the tractors are working at the pull, Buddy." Daddy veered off to the right at the gate where we met Tiny Tilley. He owned Tilley's Farm Implements and was the fire chief of Springrock. He was a fun-loving man who always had a smile and cared about his community. Tiny organized the Muscular Dystrophy festival every year and was always helping people less fortunate than himself. I remember going to the carnival one Labor Day because I had saved my week's allowance of two dollars. I had a friend that had MD and wanted to contribute because I knew there wasn't a cure yet. Tiny saw me and asked if I would speak on stage because donations weren't rolling in as he'd hoped. After being introduced by Tiny, I became frightened because people were gawking at me like I was an alien from outer space. I broke down and cried because I was scared. Tiny felt awful about using me to try to get people to open their hearts and pockets. He offered to buy me a snow cone because he wanted to see me smile again, but I just wanted to go home and sit on Daddy's lap. I forgave Tiny. He was a good man, but I have never forgotten feeling like a beggar. The looks of pity made me determined not to be showcased in that manner.

Tiny sat on a cart yakking to Cooter, who sat on a steerloader with concrete cubes hanging from a chain attached to the bucket. Tiny got up from his seat to assist Cooter to place the swaying block in the right position on the box of the sled. Tiny moseyed over to give instructions to Daddy. Cooter climbed out of the bobcat and sauntered to where we were. He had on a Massey Ferguson cap covered in grease from repairing his machines. He owned a hog farm a quarter mile from us and rented the field surrounding Spruce Knoll. I always liked Cooter because he gave me rides in his tractor and combine when he was working our acres. He was a fireman too. His white teeth gleamed because the lights were beginning to come on. I giggled, listening to Daddy and Tiny exchange information in case there was an emergency on the track.

I jumped. A loud *boom* was heard because a chunk of cement hit against steel, making the earth shake. Daddy asked Tiny, "Where do you want us?" I was excited, almost hyperventilating.

Tiny turned his face to spit a wad of phlegm into some goldenrod by the rusty sheet metal fence. He spun back around and said, "Go straight across and inside the oval. Park anywhere along the guardrail. Just be available if we need you. These suped-up engines are always dangerous. Just a little spark and we have an explosion. But Trey loves it." He was looking at me and I was grinning.

"Yes, he does. Okay then, I'll be in the area." Daddy shifted into gear and I squealed like a pig. "Here we go, Buddy."

Tiny gave a rap on the tailgate. The truck galloped over

a foot-high bump of topsoil to the clay surface and leaped up again to the grass infield. Daddy hung a left past the ambulance, a lime tanker fire truck and a green four-wheel drive truck used to fight grass fires. We crept along the hard packed ground looking for an open spot. "Daddy, fire engine green?"

"Because green is more easily seen at night." He found a vacant slot and threw the Ford into reverse, but slipped only halfway. "I'll be right back." Daddy stepped out to pry open the endgate to detach the wheelchair from the bed. I was watching the contestants unloading their tractors from flatbeds or adjusting iron weights onto the front and rear wheels. Diesel fumes engulfed the air, creating a dense black fog over the entire track. My favorite smell was exhaust from anything that ran or dug holes. Daddy came back and gunned the motor to finish parking up against a steel barrier anchored to posts cemented in the soil. He went around to get me out. "Come to Papa," He undid my seat belt and I leapt into his waiting arms. He hoisted me onto his broad shoulders and carried me to the rear bumper like he was Hercules. Daddy lifted me above his head and placed me in my wheelchair loosely. I felt I was falling, but he quickly jumped on board to better pull me up in the chair and fasten me in. "Are you comfy?"

"Yea." Daddy rechecked the brakes on the manual chair. I was five feet off the ground, and it could have been disastrous had I fallen. "I'll go get us some chow." I flashed my big grin as he skipped down the tailgate to begin his jaunt to the concession stand.

"Okay" I watched Daddy disappear in the midst of

smoke, pickups, tractors, loaders, trailers and people. I thought I was on a mini-platform because there was so much to see. My attention was diverted from Daddy to individuals searching for their seats in the bleachers underneath a sheet-metal overhang. Most people had drinks or some kind of entree in their hands to gobble on. I gazed at the spectators bantering among themselves behind a wire mesh fence, which was bolted to a retaining wall running along the track. The top of the steel grid was curved inward toward the crowd, making the fans appear to me like caged animals behind the fence. A road grader was smoothing out the runway, and a farm tractor pulled a stone boat weighted with concrete to create a packed playing surface. Every fifty feet on both sides of the track were reinforcement rods, marking the increments of feet for estimated measurements. Each metal stake had a painted white block of wood screwed on the tips with black numbers from fifty to three hundred equally spaced down the path.

    I almost hopped out of my chair because the PA system gurgled and gulped when the announcer tested his microphone. "One, two, three. Testing, testing, test." I relaxed myself after the noise was gone and regained my balance in my seat. A rickety red and white plywood shed sat in the center of the infield beside the protective railing. I glanced at the silver and gold trophies perched on the window sill. They had miniature tractors displayed on their tops. I dreamed I won one of these prizes, because I always wanted a trophy like it in my bedroom to go on my shelves of farm toys. I loved the sparkly shine that reflected off the prizes because it meant someone did something well and was rewarded for his effort. The announcer started to speak. "Ladies and Gentleman welcome to the Forty-Sixth Annual Trenton County Fairgrounds Truck and Tractor Pull. We have farm, super stock, souped-up tractors and pickups revving up and ready to pull with all of their might." The speaker droned on about the rules of the contest, but my concentration was glued to the massive hunk of steel at the starting line.

A hook and chain connected to a giant iron sled bit into the chalked clay, marking the start. On the back was a seat where a potbellied man named Tom sat to press and tug the levers controlling a steel box loaded with bars of cement. I always remember Tom because he ate two whole chickens by himself at the firemen's picnic. The kids of all the firemen loved him because he had a huge mouth, and the children stuffed marshmallows in his gaping mouth to see how many would fit. The number was twenty-five. I always called him Teddy Bear, because one time he held me on his big soft lap when Daddy was cleaning the hoses, and I fell asleep. He worked for a paving company and his job was to drive the roller on freshly laid asphalt. Tom's task tonight was to adjust the speed of the pulley to move the iron parallel beams at a forty-five degree angle. A pair of tires was on both sides of the sled underneath the weight compartment. My focus was trained on a Massey front-end loader going up the track to park next to a White tractor hooked to the roller. The line was being limed by a man to mark the finish.

My gaze shifted to a newly cut hay field outside the oval. Round, firm green bales were scattered here and there and looked like boogers to me. A railway track passed in the distance with a series of pale cement silos and elevators to grain cars. Corn was spilling into a gray boxcar from a shoot attached to one of the storage bins. All of the activity taking place before me was almost too much to witness, but I had to see everything. My head became a tennis ball volleying between the sights and sounds happening before me. I riveted to my right and saw Daddy approaching. He had two mustard-covered corndogs in his right hand and his left held a couple of paper cups. Daddy smiled at me, but I had turned toward the runway because a thick black stream of smoke sprewed out of a stack. *Vavarooom!* The International roared down the track as clumps of clay flew about. The tractor's front wheels popped up from the ground and jackknifed to the right. I screamed, "Go *IH*!" I loved International because my favorite color was red. I thought red made the tractor more powerful in some way. The rear tires dug craters, splashing dirt into the air. A man ran out, waving a white flag to signal the driver to stop. The weight in the sled had stopped the movement of the tractor. The contestant cut the motor and the front end bounced down hard on the soil.

"Just in the nick of time, I see." Daddy scurried aboard, somehow juggling our food without spilling. He then shoved one of the frankfurters into my mouth after setting the lemonade on the floor. I ripped off a bite. Mustard oozed down my chin, stinging me a bit. Daddy was wolfing his dog down, making it easier to feed me. I chewed away when the measuring gang brought out their twine, a measuring tape and a screwdriver. This was the most boring part of the pull because it was all silent and none of the machines were working. How dull, I thought, but then the tractor rocked out of the holes and retired to the infield, where gray smoke hovered. I saw a four-wheel drive John Deere being hitched to drag the sled back to the start. "Here you go." Daddy gave me another chunk to eat.

Daddy took a napkin from his pants pocket to dab the yellow substance on my lower lip. "Daddy, *IH* get chance?"

"Yes. Because he was the first puller and was testing out the conditions for the others." Daddy stuck the half-eaten dog in my mouth again and I clamped down. "Be careful with the next bite because of the stick, Buddy." The pointy end was peeping out of the meat portion of the corndog. (I remember one Thanksgiving biting into a wine glass that held an appetizer because my teeth clenched hard. I shattered the entire rim. I had glass in my mouth, but I spat the shards out without much blood. It shocked my parents and sister. After I was cleaned up, we resumed our feast like nothing had happened.)

I nodded and chomped away, watching the loader race over to fill the pothole. The tractor pounced on the mess like a kitten leaping on a counter for a scrap of meat. The bucket was forced into the earth because the front wheels were jacked up from the ground. The loader scraped the dirt into one of the craters and was raised again to repeat the same process for the other pothole. Waiting in the wings was the roller to mash the loose spot down. I took another bite. The stone boat took a second swipe at the unstable area, making it compact. I felt like I was in a sandbox pretending I was overlooking a construction site.

Daddy reached for my lemonade and tossed in a flexible straw between the slices of lime and lemon. "Want a sip?"

"Yea, plee-ase." He lifted the cup to my face and held it before me. I began to chug down the clear tangy liquid, making my lips pucker. Ice cubes sloshed around because my head bobbed and jerked.

"Not all at once. It's not going anywhere." I let go of the blue and white tube. A John Deere was puttering straight down the track as if pulling a wagon rather than a three ton hunk of iron. The tractor was sending out smoke signals. One black puff ascended followed by a pause, and then another black puff. In the middle of the performance, the green monster came to an abrupt stop and died. The weight compartment creeping on the parallel beams had become too much. Daddy tugged off the last piece of corndog and gave the burned end to me. I was smiling again. I had an infectious grin that couldn't be easily erased.

I sighed when the chain crew went about their work on the clay surface. One stuck a screwdriver into the soil at the base of the sled. (It reminded me of when Mom takes my temperature to see if I have a fever.) He unhooked the chain from the rear while two men wrapped baling twine between the 200 and 250 stakes to mark where the John Deere had quit. The steel horse was hauled back to the starting line and the last contestant sputtered toward the exit. The twine was taut between the stakes. A man dashed out from the sidelines with a measuring tape and legal pad. He measured the difference between the screwdriver and the first string to calculate the distance. A second check was taken before he scribbled on his paper. It was like watching Daddy recheck his measurements several times before sawing a stud. I always hated measuring because it was uninteresting, but Daddy said it was necessary in order to fit the board correctly in place. If something didn't move or roar, I became bored. The man reread the dimensions before he retrieved a walkie-talkie bulging from his pants pocket and radioed the figures to the booth.

I was focused on the front-end loader and stone boat going about their dirty business after the chain gang had gathered up their crude instruments. An old man in bib overalls approached Daddy and had something green in his chubby hands. A corncob pipe drooped from his rotting blackened teeth, spilling fragments of tobacco over the gentleman's girth. He wore a red hat that covered his overgrown gray hair. He looked like Frosty the Snowman to me. He gasped and grunted before depositing a crisp five dollar bill in Daddy's right palm. Daddy was stunned by his action. "For the poor cripple. Buy him something."

"We can't accept this, sir. It's nice of you to offer, but it isn't right." The man shrugged and raised his left hand in protest. I listened to the announcer, but I was wondering what Daddy and the old man were talking about.

"The run by Paul Jarrot was 234 feet and 3 inches. Next up is Lou Rosa, followed by the International of Gary Jud, who elected to forego his first try and have another go at the gold. Folks, the Food Palace has icy Cokes and jumbo dogs and drumsticks for a buck fifty…" He went on with his spiel, but I was eavesdropping on Dad's conversation now. I always thought I had to know everything that was happening. Strands of drool hovered on my lips and dropped to soak my shirt.

"Look at the poor boy. He can't even swallow or walk. I feel sorry for you. May God bless him and you." The man had tears in his eyes and waddled toward the empty flatbeds, where he took out his white handkerchief to blow his nose.

Daddy folded the money in his wallet and hoped that I hadn't heard. But I had. My drenched lips begin to purse into a pout and I was about to cry. "Daddy, am I nothing?" What I didn't understand at the time was the man meant well. It made me feel as if I was less human in some way.

"Listen to me." I stopped bawling and looked straight up at him. "Some people don't know how to react to a person like you in a wheelchair because they only see the outside. What they miss is the charming and intelligent self that I love. You have Cerebral Palsy, Buddy. CP affects your speech, your muscles and it is why you drool. No matter what individuals say or think, always remember you have a mind, and Amber, Mom and I love you." (I have since learned to accept the seemingly noble intentions of others, but I still feel different, as if I don't belong or fit into the outside world. I ignore the looks of pity and go about my life because I'm not going to hide in a closet and wait to die.) Daddy gave me another sip, and droplets of sweet water escaped from my mouth, falling onto my bare, knobby knees, gluing them together.

I chugged down most of the rest and let go of the straw, gasping for air. After I regained my breath, I glanced toward the start where a Minneapolis-Moline stood to pull. "Hey look," I exclaimed. A spool of barbed wire was contorted over the engine and around the base of the chassie. The smokestack had duct tape wrapped over twine to hold the exhaust pipe in an angled position. The tractor's tires clung to the sandy earth. The rubber was half-inflated as if a panther had stuck claws into each. The exterior frame had a yellowish-brown tint, similar to the color of urine when I had diarrhea. Every part of the machine quivered like a bowl of jello. It appeared ready to collapse at any moment. Steam bubbled from the radiator and drops of water landed on the packed ground to form a puddle.

"And now I give you the *Junkpile* ridden by Lou Rosa." The gravelly voice of the speaker rung through the night sky. The flagman motioned Rosa to begin his pull. The tractor idled for a long time without any sign of life.

There was a murmur and a snicker from the crowd, doubting that the mass of metal would ever move. "He no go. Because won't," I said to Daddy, kneeling beside me.

"Don't be too quick in your judgments now." I didn't know why Daddy was being stern, but in hindsight, I was a symbol of the *Junkpile,* because not many people thought I could succeed at anything. Suddenly the four tires rotated slowly like a water wheel at a mill continuously turning. The Minneapolis-Moline went straight ahead down the runway, but nothing could stop it. Tom tried all of the gears on the sled to make the box climb higher to halt Rosa. He was dumbfounded. The tires of the tractor shuffled over the streak of lime at the finish, carrying the white powder into new territory. The nose of the sled broke the plain. The flag man waved his right hand directing Lou to quit. It was like he was plowing a furrow in a field. He gently nudged the brakes with his left foot. The motion of the wheels just died.

"A full pull by the *Junkpile*," barked the announcer to the stunned spectators. Amid the applause I sat befuddled by what had happened before my eyes. I gawked at Daddy in astonishment. I had been a disbeliever like the amazed crowd. How had that scrap heap called "the *Junkpile*" defied the odds? "I-I-I no believe. How, why did RaRa. Go all way, Daddy?" (If I had only known the numerous inner and outer conflicts facing me in the years to come I would have rooted for the Minneapolis-Moline to win. I would be thrown into the fire to see how strong I was.)

The track was being prepared for the last try by Jud. Daddy was gazing at a twinkling star beyond the grain elevators against the ashen night sky. I was relaxing in my chair when he pointed to a gleaming object. I didn't know quite what to make of the small light at first glance. He was always making me aware of the universe around me. "You know that stars grant wishes, Trey?"

"Yeah, Daddy. I do." My head was sandwiched between the tanned arms of Daddy, and he showed me the precise star he had chosen to make his wish .

The smoke was lifting a bit, causing the star to become more luminous. "I made a wish for my Buddy." I grinned my big wide smile that I was known for. I wanted to know the secret. "All right, I'll reveal my dream for you, even though I shouldn't. Knowing you as I do, you'll ask a thousand times until you get an answer to your question. In the process, you'll drive me loony. My hope for you is that you will have the gumption and the fight that the

Junkpile had to overcome the many challenges in your life. Always remember: Hard work pays off and never give up because some people will doubt your abilities. Buddy, I love you." He bear hugged me and planted a warm smack on my left cheek.

"Okay, I will. I love you." I didn't know how difficult my life would be because I always thought everything would stay the same. I took Daddy's words to heart and stored his advice in my photographic mind. I had an amazing talent for remembering dates, quotes, names and places because I wasn't able to use my hands to write them down. I trained myself to memorize information. I could recall facts when I needed to, like a computer's data bank.

"The *Crow* by Gary Jud is ready again for another go, ladies and gentlemen." Daddy and I watched the shiny red tractor bellow out a black tornado from its stack. The front leaped skyward and the tires teeter-tottered on the axle. Clogs of dirt fiercely splattered off the rear wheels like a dust storm. A smell of oil and burned rubber engulfed the surroundings as the red machine sped onward. I almost thought the earth was rocking before me because of the shattering, thundering noise. The finish was in sight and the International was about to flip over backwards. A spark flew out from somewhere in the engine. It was like black magic had made the roaring go poof in the night. In an instant, the radiator and the front wheels slammed against the compacted clay, serving as a brake to bring the tractor to a standstill.

When the sand cleared, it was apparent the chalk line was underneath the chassis. The announcer shouted to the fans, "The winner is Lou Rosa with the *Junkpile* and second place goes to Gary Jud. Give it up for these guys for a helluva of a rip-pulling time. In ten minutes the Super Stocks will make their appearance, which is always a bang-up good time. Now folks, don't forget about Fran's Food Palace just waiting for you. Get your fill of franks and..."

I was thinking about the tortoise and the hare while I leaned on Daddy's shoulder. I was yawning and egging on the hare to beat the tortoise because he was ugly, but he kept slowly moving. Now I know why the tortoise always won the race. He didn't care what anyone said or thought of him. "Daddy, I will do good. Because I want you. Be proud of me. I love you." I yawned again.

Daddy patted my hair softly, "I already am, Buddy. Proud of you. I just want you to always believe in yourself. Promise me?" (I have carried this memory through the years and have used it when something seemed impossible to accomplish.)

"I will always, Buddy." I was getting sleepier as I listened to diesel engines purring like cats around the track. I rested on Daddy's chest. He was still gazing at the star and I was dozing, but I could hear Daddy faintly talking to someone. " Please just give him a chance in life and the strength to overcome the many barriers, both physical and emotional. Amen." I believe he had tears in his eyes because his face was wet when Daddy bent down to kiss me. Afterward, he sat, staring into the glittering beyond.

Chapter Four

The tan van coasted down a steep hill in front of the red brick school. Mom waited for the signal light to turn green again at the foot of the incline. I was looking at my school, sitting on a slope. A sidewalk led to three steps to a series of glass doors. Silver iron lettering was etched above the entrance and said *Watson Elementary School*. The American flag blew in the wind, making the rope clang against the metal pole. *Ding, ding, ding.* Young saplings tied to metal stakes driven into the ground had been planted in the open space between the street and the building. Classes weren't in session yet. It was early August.

I sighed when Mom veered to the right after the light switched to green. We drove past a line of elms ensnared in a chain link fence, serving as a boundary separating the school from a mental hospital that looked like an English castle. The van cruised slowly down the patched pothole surface and worn pavement. I saw soda cans, candy bar wrappers and empty bags of potato chips strewn in the grass among the decaying leaves from last fall. I didn't understand why people discarded items after their use or purpose was no longer valued. Mom made a hairpin turn past the east wing of the school. I wasn't allowed in that entrance because I was a disabled child requiring special care. Cars were slanted underneath the plate glass windows. On the other side was a landing for the delivery of food. Empty bread trays were stacked against the chimney.

She drove over the painted white outlines of hopscotch on the newly paved surface. To my left was the athletic field that was built on a mound like a raised pile of soil at a landfill. Concrete stairs led up the slope; in the southwest corner was a softball diamond that had a batting cage cemented to the ground. Ivy covered the fence around the outskirts, and a scoreboard leaned against the green background. By the steps was a jungle-gym in the shape of a square hotel. I thought it was more like a prison cell because of the iron maze. Crab grass hung stubbornly to the footings. The inside was naked. No children were playing on the vertical and horizontal bars. The van lurched forward to a ramp with plumbing tubing on both sides of the raised incline to prevent chairs from rolling off. I can remember the school district redoing the ramp several times because the pitch was too high and didn't meet building codes. Mom stopped by the platform and went around to the sliding door to open it.

She unraveled a pair of steel runners from the side like iron tracks on a trailer for a bobcat or motorcycle. Mom lunged inside for me. A set of clamps was screwed into the bare plywood glued to the floor. This was an invention of Daddy's to securely hold my manual in place. Mom drove me everyday to school. We lived twenty miles out in the country, and Watsons Elementary was the only school designed for special-ed students. Mom pressed her left foot down on the lever to release the hook around the chrome frame. She performed the same routine on the second clamp. I was giggling at Mom because I was always teasing her or any female. (I love to get a rise out

of women because I'm a troublemaker sometimes.) "What's so funny, Mister?" She took the handlebars and zoomed me down by a push from behind.
The wheels hit the even, black surface. "You got a bug. Your face." She used her hand to wipe her entire face only to find nothing but increased laughter from me. "I got you." She put on my brakes while white fluffy balls floated in the air from a cottonwood by the monkey bars and swing set. The fluff gathered in corners, cracks and around the playground equipment.
"All you do is tease me. Well, I'll kiss you and leave a smudge of pink lipstick on you in front of Mrs. Lewis." She folded the ramp and slammed the door shut. Mom unlocked the wheelchair and peeled up the gradual slope to the landing.
"I dare you." I had a habit of daring Mom and Amber because I wanted to see how far I could push them and see who would break first. Mom placed one foot under the right wheel to hold the chair steady and yanked the metal handle of the door open. She used her other leg as a back stop. She pushed me skillfully through the space without a single scratch. Mom had learned the fine art of navigating me around. Most of the time, people were unavailable to help open doors. A second door inside had to be negotiated in the same fashion. A snow shovel was propped against the wall, and an empty coffee can for salt sat on the window sill. I saw a spider spinning a network of string on the dusty casement, hoping to trap an insect in his web.
"I will kiss you if I want to because it's a mother's privilege and a son's duty." She briskly glided the chair

down the dim corridor, moving over the black and white chessboard tiles past Mrs. Harris' physical therapy room.

"Oh, yea. Daddy says women. Always win. Why?" We went by two rooms with orangish carpet. A teenage boy stood in the threshold of one room waving a straw in his left hand like he was a band conductor. He pranced and sang "Teeeeehaaateehaa." His eyes were glazed over and he was laughing uncontrollably. I nodded my head to the young man but he scurried behind a paneled wall because he was frightened of me or anyone. I was scared of the boy too because he looked like a lumberjack. In fact, I remember every Arbor Day two of the autistic giants were handed shovels to dig the hole for the new tree. The janitor stood, watching them as though he were a sheriff supervising prisoners working landscape duty. The rest of the student body planted the sapling after the Paul Bunyans had been hidden safely away in their room. It was thought better that they weren't seen or heard by the normal children. But it was all right with the school principal for the boys to perform hard physical labor.

"Your father was right. Women have to keep men on their toes or you guys would become impossible to live with." I grumbled something under my breath because I didn't want to lose to Mom, but I knew I would anyway. The wheelchair rolled forward past the vanilla colored cinder block walls approaching a third pair of doors. Mom curved the chair's progress toward the left door that was wide enough for walkers, canes, crutches and wheelchairs to pass.

We went into the mustard-tinted classroom between interior dividers. I can still remember the room vividly because I lived, ate, played and learned in Mrs. Lewis's class for five years. The only time I was allowed out of the room was for physical therapy. We wove around a maze of moveable partitions made of pressed wood. The exterior wall had a large window running the length of the room and segments of glass could be opened to let the cool breezes in. A banged-up radiator was underneath the window. A chubby, big busted woman with black curly hair stood by some cabinets stapling cardboard leaves onto a bulletin board. She dropped a gold leaf on the brown floor. I snickered. I loved it when Mrs. Lewis made a mistake. She kept on working as if I wasn't there and spoke to me. "I know that laugh anywhere and it must be Trey."

"How do you know?" I had a bewildered look on my face and wondered how women knew everything. I was watching her from a table in the middle of the room.

She continued punching metal staples into the cork without looking at me. "Because I have eyes in the back of my head." I believed her. She could be on the other side of the room and know what I was up to. (Usually I was laughing or daydreaming.) "I have been teaching you for five years now. I know every one of your tricks, like replacing the animals in Old McDonald's Farm with farm implements." I giggled again. She jumped off the counter and came over to hug me. "You know, Pat," she said to Mom, "I had to go to the city library to check out a book about heavy machines because I didn't know what a bobcat or a backhoe was. He is always talking about tractors and combines." Mrs. Lewis and Mom sat down next to me. I enjoyed being the center of attention because

BUDDY WHY

I always had to share Mrs. Lewis with my disabled classmates, who required TLC too.

"He is always outside watching our neighbor, Cooter, work the fields. Cooter leases our tillable acres and he steals Trey for a ride of plowing or harvesting without telling me. So, I don't panic now when I see an empty wheelchair on the knoll overlooking the backyard." (By the age of ten, I had ridden every piece of farm equipment except for a steerloader. It was too small.)

Mrs. Lewis's pearly teeth showed through her red lips, "How wonderful for Trey. Well, I have a surprise for my sixth grader this year." My eyes lit up in anticipation. It reminded me of the song for Heinz 57 Ketchup, "It's making me wait," while the ketchup slowly oozed from the bottle. "Before you become unglued," Mrs. Lewis continued, I have decided to have your desk moved to the head of the room by the chalkboard and the door. But you must promise me that you won't daydream all of the time and watch people go by." She circled me around a bit so I could check out my new digs. I saw a neat stack of books arranged on a flattop table in the far left corner leaning against the chalk tray. The alphabet was sprawled above the black slate in cursive writing. My wooden polished desk sparkled almost like when sun rays hit off a newly waxed car. Mrs. Lewis was motionless, waiting for my final pronouncement.

"I will take it."

"You drive a hard bargain, sir. Let's shake on it." She extended her right and took my clenched right fist. We shook on the deal like two gentlemen shaking after finalizing a purchase of land. "Your mother is a witness."

Mom was grinning at Mrs. Lewis. Looking back now, I'm amazed how Mrs. Lewis treated her special-ed class with dignity and respect. She was in charge and she knew the personalities of her students. In a way we were her children. "Will you excuse us? I have to talk to your mother privately."

I had an astonished expression on my face and blurted out, "But how I be in trouble? I just got here!" Mrs. Lewis and Mom laughed, because when I was bad they held conferences in the hallway after school and decided my punishment. They stood up from the low table that made Mrs. Lewis and Mom appear to be oversized dwarfs.

"I can see you are already your worrywart self. You're off the hook this time. It's nothing to be concerned about. I assure you." She ran her fingers through my thick black hair to calm my overactive imagination. "I'll be right back with two people I want you to meet."

The ladies headed for the door. "Okay, what do I do here?" They paused for a minute at the threshold and turned back toward me.

"Just admire the handiwork I have done to the place." I laughed. Nothing about my home away from home ever changed much except for the knickknacks that Mrs. Lewis made or brought.

Mom blew a kiss to me. "Be good honey. I'll see you in awhile. I love you." On Mom's left hand was a faint pink imprint and she held her spread palm out in my direction.

"Yuck. You em-bar-rass me." I screamed and raked my hands across my pudgy face to prevent the gross goobers from invading me. I was busy swatting myself while the amused women vanished before I noticed the quietness of the room. The only sound was a clock ticking to break the maddening solitude of the place I had grown accustomed to through the years. I took sighed deeply and surveyed my surroundings for the umpteenth time in my life. Beneath the clock and a few feet from a door was a three sided square of pressed wood, four feet tall by seven feet wide. Inside, a sheet of formica about two and a half feet in height had been nailed to the inner-most panel of the cube. A cutout had been carved out of the plank top to fit a person in a wheelchair. In bold gray read, "The Isolation Booth." The chamber was punishment for a bad child or a heart-to-heart talk with Mrs. Lewis. I chuckled because I remembered my frequent visits to the hole, like when I threw temper-tantrums or was defiant toward Mrs. Lewis. I was bad sometimes because I was bored and restless, since Mrs. Lewis was the only adult caring for us. I vowed to steer clear of the imposed confinement this year.

Beyond the holding cell were more tables for students. An alcove was built into the cement wall, and a metal bar hung across the vacant space. Coat hangers dangled from the pipe to the height of a small child. Laminated blue tiles had been laid on the floor of the coat rack to dry winter boots and ponchos. I always thought of locker room shower stalls when looking at the blue rectangles of the alcove, because it was hidden from view. A wooden shelf above the iron rack was used to store lunch boxes, mittens, gloves, hats, caps and toys brought by the class for Show and Tell. My eyes shifted to a large pine crate angled toward the center of the room, providing a bird's-eye view of each direction. Papers and lesson plans cluttered the desktop sitting on four pegs that reminded me of a pallet box used to pick apples. The front and sides had pink flowers from *Fantasia*. I was sick of looking at the girlish design year after year. I always had ideas that pop into my head and one was to buy a roll of more manly wallpaper for her desk by using my week's allowance. I presented the gift to Mrs. Lewis, but she installed the brown and white stripped pattern inside the isolation cage. I was told I could see my masculine paper whenever I desired.

A hickory chair was behind the desk and had a solid, shiny back. I thought it was a judge's or king's throne. To my left was a partition made of oak that separated the far corner from the rest of the room. More tables and small wooden chairs were hidden behind the movable wall. In back, lined cabinets were recessed along the floor and above. Plain metal knobs on the doors looked like triggers to maple syrup dispensers. On the counter were Chinese checkers, tic-tac-toe, pick-up sticks, *Life*, *Monopoly*, Lincoln Logs and several decks of cards. In the cupboards were art supplies, carbon paper, feeding utensils, bibs, paper towels, dish soap and sucking cups with flexible straws. The daily necessities for the children.

My vision was directed to an open area dividing the room in half. On the left was a closet for textbooks, medical supplies and a spare wheelchair for emergencies. I wondered if the poster of the freckle-faced boy still hung on the bathroom door. I always loved the red haired boy leaning on a cane and trying to grab hold of a cluster of stars beyond his out-stretched arms. He had a look of awe in his sea-blue eyes at the twinkling lights. A caption underneath him summed up perfectly, "Always reach for your dreams." I didn't know what the meaning of the phrase meant, but I gradually learned its significance. I gazed at the sink under the unfinished billboard, depicting the colors of fall above more drawers. On a metal tray over the faucet was a bar of soap. To me it appeared to be a stick of butter because of the yellowish tinge. Hand lotion and a can of Comet stood next to a stack of brown paper towels for cleaning. In the cabinets were an array of toiletries: male and female urinals, tampons, diapers, Lysol, a plastic bucket for vomit, a first aid kit with iodine and bandages. In the far right corner of the cupboard, rolls of toilet paper, disinfectant, rubber gloves and spare clothes had been set aside for the occasional accident by a student.

 I heard steps behind me shuffling on the linoleum, worn from the pounding of wheels and the jarring of crutches. It reminded me of an entrance to a construction site where heavy trucks deliver steel, concrete and lumber. "I'm back with my two friends. Did you miss me?" I saw a lady and a man accompanying Mrs. Lewis to the table where I was sitting. I was bored because I was watching the mobiles intermittently strung on the white plastic ceiling. In my imagination the two rows of lights that went across the room were a large pair of cookies with white chocolate frosting.

 "Yea, I did." I was being flip, and Mrs. Lewis responded by bopping me gently on my left arm.

 "All right, character. I see you haven't changed much. Have you?" I laughed uncontrollably for about a minute or two and peered up at the onlookers. I gazed at the young woman, wearing a navy dress that had a white collar, and I thought she was a sailor in panty hose. Her glasses were about to fall off her tiny nose, but the curly cropped blonde hair kept the tan rims in place. The man stood, holding a brown attaché case under his right arm. He had on a striped blue shirt and maize dress pants. His bifocals gave him the appearance of being a professor or lawyer. The rims of the gentleman's glasses wrapped around his head. I regained my composure somewhat before introductions were made. "Trey, this is Miss Mayes and Mr. Lindstrom. This is Trey, my creative pupil. He is one of a kind."

"How are you?" asked the young lady. She was cute, I thought, because she had round breasts and great legs. She and the man sat down at the table and Mrs. Lewis stood by me.

"Okay, I guess. So, what up?" I requested. My eyes shifted back and forth like windshield wipers swishing during a rain storm.

"They are going to ask you some questions, Trey."

I began to moan because I knew this was the same test I had taken every year since kindergarten. The questions were always the same and I was sick of taking the Piat exam, because I didn't see its purpose; but I did it grudgingly. I was staring outside at the slide and teeter-totter, while the man and the woman unpacked their testing booklets, legal pads, pencils and pens. "I have to leave the room, but I'll be in and out." Mrs. Lewis peeked at her wristwatch to check the time. "I have to pick up Darcy from speech. Will you be okay?" She was worried about me. I had become motionless without answering her.

A muffled squeak of, "Yea, go" came from me. I was being stubborn and moody because I hated the test, and remained distant. Mrs. Lewis left the classroom rapidly, glancing back at the silent scene happening with the three of us. The man set out a box that looked like an ice cream sandwich, but there was no vanilla filling the holes, just winding circles of thin tape. My concentration was diverted to a retaining wall holding back a stand of trees on a sparsely covered slope with ivy beyond the playground equipment. Gangs had spray painted foul language on the cement that read "fuck you" and "pot." I always wondered what the terms meant. All I knew was the words were bad. Every year the janitor tried to slap white-wash over the sayings in full view of the special-ed room. But in a week or two, the dirty messages would magically reappear over night and were bolder than before. When I was bored or nervous, my mind would replay the catchy rhythm of "fuck you" over and over again.

"Let's begin, shall we?" said Mr. Lindstrom to his assistant. My sight turned toward Miss Mayes holding a No. 2 pencil in her right hand and a steno pad in the other. In front of the middle-aged man was a folder; he was reading loose papers. I was getting anxious and broke the hush cast over the room because I felt like I was attending a funeral. I have never been good at being quiet for a long period of time. "What are you writing?"

Miss Mayes and Mr. Lindstrom exchanged stunned looks, but chose to dismiss my question. I knew they were writing about me and I decided I had a right to know.

"You are writing about me. Why?"

Miss Mayes coughed, "Well, yes I am, Trey. Because this is a test of your motor skills and IQ."

"Oh, I see. What's the purpose?" Again the man and the woman were aghast by my inquisitiveness, but they resumed their mundane duties and ignored me. I was antsy because this was dull, and my reaction was to grit my teeth in the direction of Mr. Lindstrom. I finally raised my voice to a high pitch and saliva arched through the air like a cat marking its territory. "Hey you. What you reading?" I demanded.

My outburst awoke the two studious individuals from their paperwork. Mr. Lindstrom glared at me. "Your record," he said in a heightened manner. It reminded me of a butler serving his master dinner. I was pleased with myself, because I had disrupted the preciseness of the examination that had to be followed in order to obtain the correct results.

"Why?"

The man was baffled by all my questions, but I was being me. He was angry. "You ask too many questions. Stop it please, Trey."

"No, I won't. Because Daddy always says to. Ask question. Because he is an engineer. He asks questions at work. He knows everything. I always ask questions. Because he says I should. Daddy is great. I sorry I ask questions. But he says it's okay. Whatever he says I do. He my hero. I love Daddy." My voice completely faded away because I was out of breath, foam hung down my chin. The two of them were dazed at my forceful independence.

The room became still once again while the two returned to their endless mound of paperwork and data collecting. I began to groan because I wanted to go home and mow the yard since Daddy would be back early from work. I was gazing at a pair of tables spaced about ten feet apart on the right side of the class beside the radiator. By the second desk was an old fashioned chalkboard in an oak wooden frame set at a forty-five degree angle, obscuring the view of the hallway. I thought the blackness of the clean slate was almost like the tar sealer that suburbanites scrape on their drives every summer to preserve the asphalt. On the other side was a single bed one could rest on if sick until a parent came. A makeshift pink curtain was draped over a taut rope connected by screw eyes to the interior wall and the trim of the blackboard for privacy. I muttered something under my breath, causing Mr. Lindstrom to stop reading his pile of sheets. "Let's begin the oral part, Miss Mayes." She quit scribbling notes and the man fished through a navy book. He then set the binder open-faced between us, reminding me of a backdrop for a puppet show.

"What are you doing?" The gentleman ran his right hand down his disgruntled face. He had grown weary of my probing. He knew I was having fun at his expense and nodded his head to the grad student to begin.

She smiled at my beaming puppy dog eyes. I was eager and waiting. "Okay, Trey. Pay close attention, please, because I'm going to ask you some questions from this book and Dr. Lindstrom will watch us. I want you to try to answer to the best of your ability. Take as long as you like. There's no rush. Do you have any questions?" Her professor had a look of disgust at any suggestion of more interrogations by me.

"No. Go, go, go, go. Because I bored." Miss Mayes laughed and Mr. Lindstrom gave a sigh of relief, and brought his sweaty palms together as if he was rubbing twigs to build a campfire.

"Okay, but take your time, Trey." I wagged my head yes. I felt I was being treated like a stupid animal. She glanced at the tablet for a second and asked, "Who was the first president of the United States?"

I blurted out, "Easy. George Wash-ing-ton. He chop down. Cher-ry tree."

"That's right. Please just answer my questions because this is a test." The man stared at me, hoping that I would conform to their rules.

"Okay, what-ever." I wasn't happy about this silly game we were playing, because I felt like I was a robot and not Trey anymore.

"Okay, Trey. How many states are there in the United States?"

"Fifty."

"Good, Trey. Who is the current president?"

"Jim-my Carter." I grumbled.

"Right. Trey, you're smart. What is the Mississippi?"

"River. Midwest." I yawned. They thought I was beginning to become tired.

"Right again. We can take a break if you want."

"No," I yelled. "I bored. Of this. Ask more. Harder please." Both of their jaws dropped at my rare request, because not many disabled children demanded difficult questions.

"By all means, Miss Mayes. Give him what he wants." The professor rubbed his goatee, waiting for me to fail.

"Okay." She looked at her mentor to make sure he wasn't bluffing. He nodded affirmatively, and she chose a question from the bottom of the list. "How much is a yard?"

"Pay loader buck-et." I said matter of factly.

"Wrong," said Miss Mayes frowning at my creative answer that had popped into my mind even though I knew the correct fact she wanted. I was just playing around and being myself. I have always loved to disprove individuals' first impressions of me, because people think that I'm a stupid moron. I was going to win the battle because I always have a trick up my sleeve.

"Pay loader, pay loader. Gravel pit. I like gravel. Because of Vaaroom. And Bang. Daddy and I. Go in pickup. Once awhile. Because we need gravel. For driveway. Guy pay loader. By big pile. He dump. A yard in pick up. Say Daddy. Because I heard him. Because his bucket. Held yard. I right." I collapsed in my wheelchair from exhaustion, but quickly recovered like a toddler who takes a cat nap and shortly wakes up, running all over.

Mr. Lindstrom scratched his scalp, pondering about something. Miss Mayes was consoling me. "It's okay. I'm sorry, Trey. But the correct response is thirty-six inches. It will be all right."

The man threw up his hands, "No, he's right."

Miss Mayes was stunned at her professor, " Uh, what?"

I laughed because I knew I had stumped them by my ingenious nature. "A week ago I had my drive paved and yesterday I received the bill from the contractor for fifteen yards of blacktop. We will give him this one, but I don't know where he comes up with these outlandish answers." I beamed over my triumph because I had won that round. I felt proud of myself for outwitting the test givers.

"Sorry, please excuse us. We have to use the little girl's room." Mrs. Lewis pushed a wheelchair by the table where the exam was taking place. The man motioned them ahead with his right palm like a flag man of a highway crew directing cars past roadwork being done. "Thank you, we won't be long." Mrs. Lewis whisked toward the back of the room.

"Hi, Darcy. How you?"

The girl meekly mouthed, "Okay, Trey," her voice barely audible. Darcy was dressed in a red jumper and satin blouse. She had on white tights and black sandals. Her pale, freckled face was hidden by Shirley Temple locks drooping down, covering her blueberry eyes.

Mrs. Lewis vanished into the small room behind the sink. I watched Darcy. I thought she was pretty, and when I saw a cute girl my mind always stopped thinking. (I still have this disease today, where my brain goes blank at a sight of a beautiful woman.) "Trey, Trey, listen to me please. We're ready to move on," said Miss Mayes.

"Oh, yea. I for-got. Sorry."

The professor and the grad student were puzzled by my aloofness, because I would be attentive one moment and not the next. I had come out of my daze again. "I'm going to ask you a sequence of numbers and I want you to come up with an answer. I can say the order only once. So, be alert."

"Okay." The squeal of footrests echoed from the rear

and was followed by a rustling of cloth being pulled down.

"Ready, Trey?"

"Yea, yea." I was getting rambunctious again.

She slowly read a series of numbers from the book in front of her. "What is three plus one plus four times three minus two divided by seven minus three?" I stared at the ceiling and my eyes were rolling around searching the answer from thin space. I heard a grunt and then a steady flow from the back. I tried to keep my mental frame of mind but I kept picturing Darcy urinating on the toilet. I almost had the magic digit in my computer.

Something just clicked in and I said "Three." The partners were amazed at my accuracy.

"Very good, Trey. You're smart," she said. The man raised his fury brows in disbelief. He was certain I was mentally challenged and he was going to prove it, but he was running out of options to place that label on me. I heard a rip and knew a swab of paper was being used to wipe the drips of urine from Darcy's loins by Mrs. Lewis. I started to have an erection thinking about the opening women had between their legs and why it made my penis grow. I wondered why God had made people different. I blushed because I was aroused and was being praised by the young lady. I felt ashamed, but looking back now, I was just being a curious boy.

"One more, Trey." I nodded for her to go on. " What is eight times eight minus eight divided by seven?" Mrs. Lewis and Darcy had come out of the powder room to wash their hands.

"Eight." They dried their hands with brown paper

towels without a sound except for the wrinkling made by the coarseness of the napkins against their skin. The wet towels were tossed in a trash can beside the counter, and Mrs. Lewis started to push the wheelchair toward the door. Mr. Lindstrom held his left hand to stop Mrs. Lewis's progress. "We're about through here. Would you send in his mother, please?"

"Okay. I will after I take Darcy to the bus. Pat is outside in their van waiting. I'll be back in a few minutes with his mom." I whispered "Bye," to the delicate doll blinking her Betty Boop's eyes at me. Mrs. Lewis lunged forward and strolled out the door, pushing Darcy.

My attention shifted again to Miss Mayes, who was wearing a slip underneath her navy dress. I caught a glimpse of white lace on her tannish knees below the hemline and I pondered why females wore soft garments like bras, panties, slips and nylons. I was embarrassed at thinking dirty thoughts about the opposite sex. My head rose up to take in what she was saying to me. "Trey, Trey, Trey, are you there?"

"Oh, oh yea," I sheepishly said, while the middle aged man glared at me, trying to figure out why I would be alert and then become despondent. I was worried that Mr. Lindstrom had seen me peeking between the woman's legs. My face turned raspberry again because Daddy always said it was impolite to peek up a lady's dress.

"Are you sick?" she asked. I was becoming redder and redder.

" No, no. I okay. I posi-tive." They shrugged, not knowing what was going on inside my demented mind.

"Just two more questions to go. Are you up to it?"

"Yea, yea. Go, go, go, go." Mr. Lindstrom nodded at his assistant to continue the examination.

"How many is a dozen, Trey?" I giggled and my eyes glittered because I was going to be clever in my response.

"Thirteen," I yelled.

" No, it's twelve."

"Yea but. Daddy and I. Get up every. Sunday early. And go pickup. To Benners Bakery. Before Ma and Amber. My dumb sis-ter." I laughed because I was joking. " Wake up. Go get dough-nuts. I always go in. Pick few. They always give. One free. Called. Ba-ker dozen. Daddy -ets me pick. Last one. Get raspb-erry. Sugar on top. Or cream fill -ongjohn. With icing. Ma gets mad. We eat about four. One. Before get back. But -eave. Choco-late ones. Amber . She -ikes them. Daddy says to. Be creative because. An en-gineer always is. I hope you don't mind. Daddy great." Miss Mayes was dumbfounded by my determination. I was grinning from ear to ear because I had them hoodwinked.

Mr. Lindstrom threw off his glasses to rub the strain from his bleary eyes. "Give him that one too. He's right again." The gentleman put his bifocals back on and bit his lip to control the burning rage inside him. "Ask the last one," he instructed the young woman in a high pitched tone.

"Trey, what do you call a kid who can walk and talk normal?"

"Reg-u-lar."

"Why. May I ask?"

"Because are. Like every-one else. Daddy and Ma say. I reg-u-lar. Per-son who happens. To be in wheel-chair.

Because Daddy says. My mind doesn't tell. My -egs and arms. To work right. Not my fault. Daddy says I. A boy. His Buddy. He and Ma. Expect good grades. By me. And be good Mrs. -ewis. Be nice to Am-ber. That's hard. Because I tease her. Make her cry." I laughed for a second. "I love Am. Ma too. Daddy is the best. Because he is great." My mouth was parched from all of my jabbering because my vocal cords had stopped functioning for now. Mr. Lindstrom and Miss Mayes were astounded at my rattling rate of speech and vocabulary. The professor and his protegé returned to their writing and reading respectively. I slumped in my chair, watching the boring silent individuals work. I thought college people were painfully dull because they always were serious.

My eyes roamed the room and I suddenly became happy when I saw Mom and Mrs. Lewis approaching the center table. " Hi, MAAAA." They smiled at my bubbly face, while the other two adults stood up to introduce themselves to Mom. She shook their hands and exchanged pleasantries. I felt like a prizefight was about ready to break out with all of the handshaking going on. Mrs. Lewis took a seat on the right side of me while the man showed Mom a chair to my left. I decided to remain silent during the proceedings, because I was afraid of saying anything wrong when the two most powerful women in my life were beside me. My curiosity was sparked because I knew the get together was about me. What was this all about, I wondered?

Mr. Lindstrom motioned the lady to begin the meeting after he sat down. "Well, I must say your son is a bright and lively character. You should be proud of Trey."

Mom grinned and I chuckled, because I had heard this kind of statement a million times by polite, disabled advocates wanting to defuse the situation until they unloaded their negative recommendations. "Thank you. My husband and I treat our son no differently than other parents would their children."

"We sure heard a lot about his father. Trey really admires him."

"Yes, they're inseparable."

"The reason we had Trey tested was to see if he could be mainstreamed with normal kids of his own age and grade. Mrs. Lewis thinks he needs a challenge and would be capable of performing in a class. What do you think?"

"That would be wonderful. I would approve, and Sam, my husband, would also." I was bewildered because I thought the ladies were talking about fishing for trout. I kept my flapper shut, and Mr. Lindstrom was inconspicuously quiet, stewing over his pile of notes.

Mrs. Lewis commented, "I strongly believe Trey would clearly benefit from attending regular classes. He needs more social interaction and mental stimulation than I can provide." She patted me on my right shoulder. "He's one of the best students I've ever had."

The young woman winked at me. "I perfectly agree with both of your assessments. He sure is a smart little man. I give my approval." She riveted toward her professor with a sharp glance. "What do you think, Dr. Lindstrom?"

Before answering, he monkeyed around by yanking off his glasses again and shuffling through his papers once more as if he were playing a bad hand of three card stud.

Mom was waiting for his ace in the hole because he had the trump card and we all knew it. But first he had to play out his hand before he revealed his pick to us. "I'll admit he is very smart. He is a creative child. I'll give you that, Mrs. Pike. You should be very proud of him. I was amazed at some of the answers he gave us. But the school board doesn't have the funding to hire an aid to be with him if he is in a normal class. And the principal of the school is concerned about being liable if he happened to get hurt. Other parents like yourself have sued school districts because their Danny-Boy fell on school grounds. Mr. Gates, the principal, thinks this special-ed class is safe and is enough for him." I bowed my head almost to my lap because I was ashamed at not being able to measure up to the professor's standards. (Times like these have often happened in my life. All because some expert's opinion is more valued by society. It's easier to conform to their way, but it's tragic. A mind IS a terrible thing to waste.)

Mom had a scowl on her face, listening intently to the man's implication. She reached for my left hand and held my long fingers in the soft cradle of her palm. "I, er, just have some reservations. I know you want the very best for him." (Sometimes I think I'm a nonexistent pronoun in some people's minds.) "And that's commendable, really. But he is a slow learner and I have to de-"

Mrs. Lewis had been studying the situation and interrupted Mr. Lindstrom's swan song. "What if the Pikes signed a waiver, making the school not liable for any physical harm that might happen to Trey?" The professor closed his eyes and probably wished that the fragile matter would dissolve away like winter's dirty snow in the spring. "Would you agree to sign a document releasing liability, Pat?"

Mom said in a strong voice, "Yes we would." She looked directly at Mr. Lindstrom. Why was there a heated discussion about me when I have never fished before? I wanted to know.

"No, I'm sorry. There is no spare aide for him. It would be unfair to other students because the teacher would have to spend more time with him. I have to use my better judgeme-" What he was saying was to be happy with small favors and let sleeping dogs lay.

Mrs. Lewis spoke up again. "I have talked to Miss Fredricks, our sixth grade teacher, about Trey. And she has offered to let Trey enroll in her U. S. history and English classes. We came up with the idea of having her students take turns helping Trey write and flip pages for him. It would be a trial run and just for two hours a day. And if it doesn't work, we'll pull him immediately out of the classes. I promise. Pat has already agreed to the arrangement." The man coughed and stared out the window without saying a word.

"You have my vote," said the young woman. "It would be a learning experience for all of those involved, including Trey." Mom and Mrs. Lewis nodded to the lady. "Oh, why not let them try, Dr. Lindstrom?"

He cleared his throat and scratched his bald head as if he had a headache, but he was looking for a way out of the mess created by the women. The professor threw up his hands. I almost thought he was being arrested for a crime, but there wasn't a policeman in sight. "Okay, okay, okay. I'll give in against my better judgment. I know when

I'm down for the count. He can attend the two classes, I guess. But I still reserve my first evaluation of him as being developmentally disab-" He snarled at his student for stirring up a hornet's nest.

"Thank you," Mom said. She wept as she embraced me. "Yucky," I shouted. Everyone laughed at my remark except for the professor who left in a huff. "Can I have. Rocky road. Ice cream. Please MAA."

Mom snuggled me as though I was Amber's teddy bear, Ashes, that she carried everywhere until the stuffed animal was rags. I was embarrassed because Mrs. Lewis and Miss Mayes watched the lovable soap opera scene. "Yes, you may. Whatever you want. We have reason to celebrate! But this is an exception for today only." I was happy because Mom was leaping up and down. Had she hit the jackpot at a casino?

"Ma you nuts. I like. Because I. Get ice cream. For nothing. What I do. Deserve? I do. Everyday to eat. Ice cream. Because I love it." The women laughed at my comments and Mom was squeezing the pulp out of me. I thought I was an orange when she made fresh orange juice every Sunday morning.

This little victory changed my entire life and allowed my parents to pursue lofty dreams for me. I became a thinking person capable of reaching new heights.

Chapter Five

Daddy was loading me into the pickup to go cut some oak for our wooden stove that heated the kitchen in our old farm house. I blinked my eyes because the sun rose through the neighboring fields of endless green. I was afraid to look at the golden circle in the sky since Daddy told me never to look directly at the sun for long. He tugged the seat belt snugly around my booster cushion and slammed the passenger door shut, making me jump. Daddy walked to the driver's side and revved the engine before rocketing down the gravel lane, leaving behind a trail of dust. I always loved riding in the truck. I was physically closer to Daddy and everything became smaller, like the farm house in the rear view mirror. We approached the country road of packed stones that reminded me of the corn flake crumb breading Mom used on chicken. The two surfaces were held together by a magic chemical. Rings of dirt swirled among the blue spruce, elm and hickory branches, floating in the open meadow and vanishing.

Daddy drove past the fenced pasture and a large field of tasselling corn danced to the rhythm of a light breeze. We sped by Fortson's red brick colonial house and I looked at the white overhang above the columns to where a black eagle was flapping its wings against the gable. The sight of the iron bird was always spooky to me. I thought something bad was going to happen. Maybe the eagle was going to carry me off to a distant land. Daddy reassured me that my overactive imagination was working too much. But I kept having visions of being alone in the truck with no one driving, screaming for help and waiting to crash. I often had these dreams, but I always woke with Daddy or Mom by my side telling me nothing would ever harm me and to go back to sleep. Daddy signaled a right as we came to a stop and turned onto a washed out lane. We jiggled in the cab while the tires kangarooed through the muddy track that had boulders appearing like marshmallows stuck between the chocolate ruts. The pickup careened down the hill to a hollow, where our woods stood on the edge of the property line. Daddy led us to a grassy spot separating the drive from the trees. Perfect for a picnic table to eat a snack or lunch. We parked next to a downed oak with its trunk still intact, the limbs and roots clinging together in a profound sleep.

"Want something before I start cutting?"

"Yea, boost please," I said, gazing toward Daddy's bifocals. He lurched over to me. I was about ready to slip beneath the seat harness and fall into the hole underneath the dash. All of the rocking had unsettled my posture. He took a firm grasp of my armpits lifted me into an erect position using his tender, giant hands.

"Is that better, Buddy?" He gave the belt another pull before climbing out the front door.

"Okay. Yea. Cut wood, Daddy." Drool squirted from my mouth, resembling flames coming from a snarling dragon. A spray of droplets rained on the windshield like a morning's mist, but the water was on the inside instead of the outside. Daddy stood next to the door and stuffed his hands into yellow workman gloves. They reminded me of the mittens Ronald McDonald wore, except Daddy's were soiled and ragged.

"Remember, if you need or want anything, wave your hands all over the place and I'll come running. Like how I taught you when you watch Cooter working in the field. Okay?"

"Yep, okay." He reached over the bed to grab the chainsaw when a thundering roar was heard echoing down the worn path. A truck that had a red bed and elevator attached for dumping silage into troughs appeared. It was our neighbor, Willy Smith, making his first round of the day to feed his beef herd. He was a beef producer and had several cattle feedlots in the area. His major operation was a mile away to the west, where he kept all of his equipment and grain. Willy owned several thousand acres of land. A hundred acres was behind our small farm. He had a barn and an old corncrib in the middle of the field to let his cows glean the pickings after the corn harvest. This would automatically fertilize the acreage by the droppings from the cattle. I remember once when all of the cows got out accidentally and the whole neighborhood helped round up the carousing animals. I enjoyed riding down Willy's easement in the truck, because I pretended I was a cowboy on the Western trail. The dark wooded valley was engulfed with the smell of rotten cherries. "Daddy, it's Willy." Daddy carried the Homelite across the open space of grass where Willy had jumped out of the navy cab of his International.

"Howdy, Sam. I see you've the little guy tagging along." Willy chomped away on a wad of spearmint gum as he shouted to me. "Hey, Trey, be good and I'll give you a ride on my dozer. We'll be chopping corn soon. We'll mow down those piles of silage, by golly." I laughed, thinking about going to Willy's farm, which sat on rolling hills of pastures. I loved to go to the open silo he had dug out of one hill behind his barns and grain elevator. Daddy and I would go over when he was chopping corn to watch the blower throw a load of green silage in an arc into the pit where Willy's bulldozer sat. After a chuck wagon was emptied, Willy would knock down the pile in three swipes and run over the fresh corn with a sheep roller to pack the loose fragments. While Willy was waiting for the next batch to be blown in, Daddy would lower me down to Willy, who maneuvered me somehow into the steel cage. Willy held me in his lap and covered my eyes with his callused hands to protect me from the falling particles of corn. My favorite part was smashing and spreading the pile. It was like molding a lump of clay into a thin, layered surface. I felt I had played a role in the enormous mountain of feed.

Daddy and Willy were exchanging words, but I was out of earshot. It drove me bonkers, because I had to know everything. I was looking at Willy's blue overalls that made him appear to be a worker at a circus cleaning up after the elephants. My attention shifted to the stand of elm, cherry, walnut and hickory. A few oak were scattered in, and pieces of jagged metal stuck to chucks of concrete mixed in the green undergrowth. Mike Fortson had used the woods for a dumping grounds for old implements, rocks from his fields and an assortment of junk like rolls of barbed wire. I always was sad to see the garbage littering the silent beauty of the trees, reminding me how life can be cluttered by nonsense affecting how we think and view living. Raspberries had begun to ripen on thorny vines entangled in the thick grass and leaves. I was amazed how everything seemed to be linked to a greater force or being.

I turned my eyes to the dead oak lying in front of me and thought a large monster had clawed the gentle giant down, leaving clumps of twigs strewn about the ground. Fresh soil had been shoved around. I noticed a pair of tracks that had made an imprint on the earth. Using the evidence present, I realized a bulldozer had pushed it down. My question now was why? I heard a door shut, causing me to jump. I didn't lose my balance.

Willy gunned the diesel engine forward under a canopy of branches toward an open gate leaning on a warped fence post with a *No Trespassing* sign. I saw a belch of blackness disappear into the corn and kept watch on the truck's rear until my vision was obstructed by the greenness. I took a deep breath to gather in the exhaust fumes I loved to sniff. I knew it was bad for my health. It was like eating too much sugar or fat, but I always enjoyed the smell I associated with tractors toiling in the fields.

Daddy ripped away at the starter three times before the saw whined. I shouted, "Hey, hey Daddy. Cut wood." He glanced over at me to see if I was all right. I was giggling to myself because I loved to laugh. Daddy proceeded to take apart the massive oak, sinking the sharp beaver-like teeth into a limb. Kernels of dust spewed from the blade everywhere. I was always amazed at how steel could separate solid wood. I watched Daddy's movements down the tree and thought the tangled branches resembled a crossword puzzle. Every cut Daddy made was another clue in solving the whole jointed entity.

I supervised the sawing from my seat as limbs were detached and fell to the ground. The saw kept gnawing at the oak slowly but evenly, as if a clock was ticking away in the dead of the night. Daddy measured the length of each log exactly, using his engineer's eye for a precise cut. I heard a rumble of tires from the distance bouncing over the gravel. My head riveted, toward the rocky lane where the mile-long cornfield started. Blue and red suddenly peeked through the greenery. "Vaaroom, I like diesel," I said to myself. When Willy drove past us, he tooted his horn twice and waved to me. I gleefully screamed and the feed truck traveled on to deliver silage for Willy's other cows.

My concentration popped back toward Daddy working away on the now naked tree. He had trimmed off all the branches, leaving only a few bare outstretched limbs hanging on the barkless trunk. Daddy heaved the saw up to his chest, pointing the blade toward the earth. He fingered a switch on the side of the motor and all at once the rattling ceased. Silence descended on the woods. The only sound was Daddy walking over the brittle twigs. I watched him carefully making his way around the maze of pieces scattered about the golden shavings sprinkled every direction. Sweat was pouring down Daddy's forehead and neck as he approached the Ford. He smiled at me before putting the tool back in the bed and opening the driver's door. Daddy stood outside the cab, admiring his work, then glanced at me. "Whew! That's hard work, Buddy."

I never knew how physically demanding cutting wood was, but I was taught by my parents to always take pride in what I accomplished no matter how small the task. (Whether it was reading a book or crawling on the floor, I was proud. I could say I did this after finishing a goal or a challenge, giving my confidence a lift.)

"Daddy, cut more."

He laughed when he sat on the blue vinyl interior of the pickup, resting his weary body. "No more today. I'm bushed." I was frowning because I wanted to keep hacking up the sleeping beast. Daddy pulled out a tissue from his pants pocket to blow his nose and took off his steamy glasses. Daddy wiped the lenses with a towel he kept in the truck for when we would be traveling and eat at a restaurant. I hated wearing the makeshift bib because I felt like a baby, but I knew it protected my clothing from food stains. "Tomorrow, we'll finish up. You can be a slave driver sometimes, dammit all."

Daddy spat on his glasses and polished the bifocals thoroughly by rubbing the rag over the lenses. I began to pout. I was on the verge of crying, but I managed to hold back the downpour for now. I was quiet while he slipped his shades back on. "I'm sorry, Buddy. I shouldn't have yelled at you. I just get-" He stopped in mid-sentence and said, "Please, forgive me. I love you, Buddy."

My sad expression was beginning to dissipate and rays of sunshine broke through the looming dark cloud. "Okay, Daddy. I get bossy. I sorry. I love you."

"All is forgiven." He slapped his right hand on my bony left knee. We sat in stony silence looking over the morning labor and the hush of the woods.

"Daddy how. Oak fall down?" My questioning eyes stared at him waiting for the secret to come out. Daddy was relaxing by leaning against the seat and taking a catnap.

He lazily said, "Because Willy asked me if he could knock down the tree with his bulldozer since it was dead." I grinned because I had used the clues at the scene to figure out a dozer had been there, but I wanted to know the reason why. Daddy kept telling his story until I was satisfied. "He was concerned about the oak coming down on top of his tractors or blocking the lane in winter. I said fine."

"Oh. Good idea. How you know. That oak dead?"

Daddy scratched his head to shake the dust from his brown hair. Grains flew in the air, creating a whirlwind inside the truck, but quickly subsided. "Well, by how the center of the tree is hollow. And by the bark being stripped off the trunk." I kept imagining a doughnut hole being something round. I didn't understand how hollowness affected the life of the oak, because the outside was still intact. I was always depressed when I bit into the empty hole of a powdered doughnut because I felt an element was missing or had been taken away. I wondered why some had holes and others didn't.

Debris had settled in the cracks of the floor board and corners of the interior. "Why do things. Die, Daddy?"

He coughed before answering me. "That's just a law of nature. All things must have an end. Even you and I will die sometime." I was stunned and confused by his statement. I felt as if a person had let out the air of a balloon floating through the blue sky. I peered out the passenger window to see a rustling among some wild flowers on the outskirts of the woods. I always believed Daddy would live forever because he was big and strong. Daddy continued talking as if I was listening, but I was more concerned about what was scurrying toward us. Was it a snake? His eyes stared at the fallen tree almost in a trance. "But you'll be around for a long time. I don't know if I will. But don't worry about it." Daddy's voice drifted off. I couldn't detect any more movement in the still, tall grass. My vision had focused on a decaying elm log with fungus covering the outer shell when suddenly the weeds next to the rotten elm began to quiver. I was frightened by the snake like motions of the grass beside the dead wood. I felt my hair rising up on its ends. I almost screamed until I saw a black head and two pointed ears appear through the green. The animal hopped onto the dead elm and stood on all fours in a statuesque pose. Its tail wrapped around its front paws. After I had regained my composure I shouted, "Daddy, it's Lic-or-ice. Daddy, Daddy, Daddyyy."

He was in a complete daze, but finally woke up to my screeches. "What, uh Buddy?"

Daddy winced while he tried to understand my broken speech. "Hey, Daddy. Lic-or-ice here." He brushed his hands across his face to stir his mental wits enough to comprehend what was going on.

Licorice, our cat, meowed at me, making Daddy look out of the side mirror. To his astonishment he saw a pair of gold circles with green dots trained on him. "Now I see what the jabbering is all about." Licorice, twitching his black wand like a pendulum, proudly surveyed us like we were his servants.

I was happy and grinned at Daddy. "How Lic get here?" I watched my black cat lick his right front paw in a rhythmic motion over his face like he was strumming a banjo for my entertainment. Licorice and I had a special bond that gradually developed over the years. When we first adopted him from an old lady who took in strays, he was Amber's cat. I had been scared of animals, but Licorice would jump up on me and purr in my ear. Other animals would be afraid of my wheelchair, but not Licorice. He had a trick of retrieving a rubber ball in his mouth like a dog, and he won me over by dropping his toy in my lap, waiting for me throw it. Licorice learned that I wasn't physically able to play with him and he never asked me to feed or open a door for him. The companionship of Licorice was going to be important down the road for Amber and me. (Especially for me, because people came and went during my life. I have met many individuals over the years who share their love with me for short periods, only to move on in their lives like a rapid current flowing by a buoy mired in muck. I always feel that I'm missing out on what other able-bodied persons take for granted, such as going out or talking on the telephone, but Licorice was always a constant in my youth.)

Daddy cleared his throat. "Cats are able to travel long distances, especially a tomcat like your friend there. Well, I'm getting hungry for some lunch. How about you?"

Daddy was smiling at me before he twisted the keys in the ignition to rev the engine. Licorice was startled by the noise and leaped into the spiraling wild undergrowth that reminded me of a jungle. "Yea, I eat. Let's go, Daddy. Will Lic be okay?" I was worried about Licorice being far away from home, but Daddy glanced into the rear view window before backing up. He throttled the gas and slowly made a reverse U-turn, then threw the Ford forward. Daddy arched to the right, heading up the muddy, bumpy hill. I enjoyed being bounced around, because riding in the truck was one of my favorite things to do growing up.

"He will be fine, Buddy. Licorice is a good hunter," Daddy assured me, and hung a left down the country road between the cornfield and Mike's manicured lawn.

We coasted down the stone pavement to the knoll. Rays of sunlight glistened off the chrome of the wheelchair that had been left on the porch. (I can still see the towering blue spruces standing amidst the endless grass and smaller trees.) Further off was the white farm house. I always thought that the farm would be where I lived forever. It was safe and it was beautiful. "Oh, what a gorgeous day, Buddy." Daddy said, merging onto the driveway. I saw tears sprinkle down his cheeks.

"Yea, I love. It too." I was going to ask him why he was crying, but before I could, he swiped the droplets away as if swatting a fly.

Chapter Six

Amber was munching on Fruit Loops at the kitchen table and slumping over the bowl to catch the drops of milk drizzling from her mouth. She was making faces at me. I was sitting across the flat oak table sucking up apple cider from a glass mug. I bent over to take a gulp now and then. After I took a breather, Daddy ran a towel over my wet chin to keep my overalls and kelly green shirt from getting damp. I always had a light breakfast, because if I ate anything before school in the morning, I would throw up. Doctors hadn't been able to explain my early morning sickness. My solution was to skip breakfast entirely, because I was tired of vomiting in the van on the way to school. Sometimes we would be half way to school, and Mom would have to turn back to change me because I had puked all over myself. Mom and Daddy agreed to my idea of a light breakfast, which worked nine times out of ten.

Daddy ate his customary two fried eggs and two slices of burnt, buttered toast covered thickly with Mom's homemade strawberry jam. Licorice was cruising around the unfinished floor. (Daddy hadn't laid the linoleum yet.) I watched Licorice prowling for food and attention. He wasn't having much success. Mom was at the counter preparing lunches for Amber and me. Open jars of mayo, mustard, horseradish and packages of meats were strewn about.

"Yellowhair. I get you." I saw Amber staring at me, miming a funny face, and I responded by gritting my teeth angrily until I lashed out.

"Don't call me that stupid name because I hate it." I was giggling because I had gotten under Amber's skin. I called Amber "Yellowhair" for a nickname. I made it up one day as I saw her walk through the meadow in a white dress. Her blonde, straw-like hair blew in the wind. (I still call her "Yellowhair," but now the name is used affectionately as a symbol of our childhood.) Licorice was meowing shrilly, making the brick walls of the old farm kitchen reverberate. His black tail stood in an erect position while he waited to be fed, standing near Mom's feet where the lazy susan held his dry and wet food. I always was surprised at how Licorice knew where his stash was, and how he always would yowl demandingly.

Mom carried over Happy Days and Mickey Mouse lunch boxes, ignoring the deafening din. She slammed down the metal containers on the stained wooden surface. "Will you two stop it right now? It's the first day of school, for heaven sakes!" Mom glared at us until we were quiet except for Licorice. I kept hearing Fonz go, "Heyyyyy," in my mind while I silently stared at Amber. I reminded myself to stay cool, or I would be in Mom's doghouse all day. Mom strutted back to the cabinets to grab a can of Super Supper from the cupboard. I was amazed at how Licorice instantly knew the sound of the sharp winding cutter carving the lid. He smacked his chops. I loved to watch his tiny tongue swiveling out of his mouth like he was a cobra about to attack a mouse. Mom took a knife from the utensil tray in the top compartment above the sink and dumped half into his dish. "There, shut up." Licorice proceeded to lick off the brown gravy from the meat portion, making the only noise in the room.

Daddy had been jotting down reminders on three-by-five index cards for work. He always wrote with a black ballpoint pen, and his handwriting was beautiful, almost appearing to be printed. I remember dictating letters to Daddy because I couldn't write myself. I'd watch him make his Bic dance across the yellow legal pad, thinking I never would. But Daddy said I would be able to write someday by myself with a computer. I thought he was nuts. He drained the last of his coffee and stole a peek at his wristwatch. "It's time to go. Are both of you ready for school?"

"I guess." I grinned at Daddy, stuffing the notes and pen in his front breast pocket. He stood up from the table and went out the screen door.

Before leaving, he kissed Amber, who was carrying the breakfast dishes to the sink. "I'll bring the van around and help load Trey today." Mom nodded to him behind the closed wire-mesh door while hustling to return the lunch materials back to the refrigerator. Licorice pounced up on the captain's chair that Daddy had been sitting on, and curled up in a ball, watching the stupid human commotion. I thought Licorice was right about how people sometimes act like a swarm of bees spinning out of control.

"Get your things together, Amber." Mom rushed over to the wheelchair to tuck the lunch box into the navy pouch behind my chair. Amber picked up her lunch and a pencil case from the table. She stood by the door in her pink and white flowered dress, and a pale ribbon nestled in her shinning blonde hair. Her sea blue eyes twinkled in the morning sunlight and radiated the natural beauty of Amber's irises.

Mom unlocked my brakes and Daddy walked in, smelling of gasoline. "All is roaring to go." Daddy held the door open and Mom tilted the chair up to push me through the entry leading to a gray cement deck. The rear tires bolted over the front step. I felt like I was riding a dolly: It reminded me of a man delivering beer into a bar. The upper half of the wheelchair was let down on the smooth concrete. Amber tagged behind us, and Daddy made sure he had firmly secured the kitchen door by yanking the knob twice. He followed us underneath the rafter of the semi-enclosed porch. A long yellow bus was seen through the quilt-work of green.

"Mommy, my bus is here." I heard the screeching of brakes. "Can I go?" Amber gazed up at Mom and Daddy pleadingly for permission to dash off to the school bus.

Red flashing lights began to blink. I thought of railroad signals blinking danger ahead.

"Okay, Sweetheart, you may go. Stop before crossing. Hear me?" Daddy warned her. "I love you." He hugged and kissed Amber.

"I love you Daddy, Mommy and Trey. Bye," squealed Amber, and she quickly ran down the gravel drive. We watched from the deck, standing beside a couple of folding lawn chairs.

"Don't forgot to look both ways," Mom shouted at Amber. I saw the waiting bus filled with screaming kids and didn't feel I was missing anything special. I knew I had to go to an accessible school, and the Springrock

District had stairs, making it difficult for a wheelchair to negotiate. I accepted it, but Mom and I did get tired of driving thirty miles each day. (I didn't know what a privilege it was for me to attend any school, because a lot of disabled children were left without any education.) Mom watched to see if Amber had listened to their instructions correctly. Daddy loaded me into the van. "I'll be here when you get home," yelled Mom, and blew a kiss to her daughter. Amber did all she was told and found a seat on the bus. The driver turned off the warning lights, and the oblong vehicle sped slowly forward along the country lane before vanishing between the fields of green.

Daddy was about to ram the side door of the van closed before Mom noticed that I had been clamped in to place. "Goodbye, Buddy. Have a great day."

Before he shut the door, I said, "Okay, I love you. Daddy. I will, bye." Daddy finally pulled the gliding panel and locked the handle. Mom buckled herself into the front seat. He rechecked the sliding door and gave Mom a peck on her cheek. She lovingly embraced Daddy before he went back to his truck directly behind us. Mom started the engine and whisked down the driveway to the road. I was watching the pickup from the rear window while Mom veered onto the pebbled asphalt. I smiled and giggled, looking at Daddy waving his right hand at me. I enjoyed playing this game, resembling Follow the Leader, going past the Fortsons and the washed out trail. We kept traveling between a forest of corn on either side of the lane.

Mom was approaching a small hill where elms lined both sides of the road. She slowed to a creep because a stop sign was at the peak, and Daddy had reduced his speed to a crawl. I had been grinning away at Daddy until I felt the van wasn't moving. I turned my head to see a two fanged monster coming right at us. On its back was what appeared to be a flame-thrower. The orange three-wheeled chopper was pulling a red wagon, followed by four International tractors, each towing a chopper box. We had to wait for the convoy to pass before we could proceed. It reminded me of ants in a line carrying grains of sand on their backs to build a hill. I was excited because I loved watching a stalk of corn being turned into bits and instantly blown into the dark opening of the wagon. I drooled when I twisted myself to grab a glimpse of farm equipment descending the beaten lane that went past our woods to Willy's cornfield and feedlot.

We surged up the shady incline to the stop where Mom paused for a moment before hanging a left on Lema Road. Daddy had climbed the slope. I was still smiling at him and he honked his horn, making me jump. Mom veered onto the two-lane highway that went to Brookdale, where my school was. As we took off down the county trunk road, I yelled, "Bye, Buddy!" I saw the truck dart straight across the double yellow line.

I sat silently looking for any farmers or construction men working, because I would pretend to do what I saw when I was alone or watching cartoons in the afternoon. It was my way of playing by myself. I'd plow a field or act as a foreman, giving orders to my road crew. "Ma I go home. Okay now." I was staring wantingly at her.

She glanced in her rearview mirror and saw I was grinning. "Why, may I ask? As if I don't know already,"

Mom said sarcastically, but kept driving the route to school.

"All the RaRa's. And wagons. I go help. I country boy. Because all diesel. I like. Corn and. Smoke flying. All over. Please Ma. I help Willy." Mom always had problems with me during harvesting and planting time, because school was the same boring pace and nothing ever changed from day to day. I enjoyed watching the farmers hustling about their work. It was more entertaining to me than being in that ugly special-ed classroom. Mrs. Lewis's class wasn't allowed recess outside for fear of one of us getting accidentally hurt. By staying home I could be outdoors, feeling I was a part of something.

"Sorry, Trey. You're going to school and that's final! You can watch when you come home. This is the end of our conversation and I don't want to hear any whining or you'll be sent to your room when we get home. No watching the tractors. I mean it," she said to the whimpering me. I was pouting, and tears were forming in my eyes. My protruding lips were about ready to drag my jaw into my lap, but Mom reinforced her position again. "I mean it, Trey."

I coughed to clear my throat and lowered my head to my sleeve to swipe away my watery eyes. I dried my pupils by myself and sat in an erect posture for several minutes, because I knew Mom always kept her word. If I didn't behave myself I would pay the consequences later. I felt ashamed of what I had done and couldn't stand being quiet for very long. "Okay, okay, okay. I sorry okay. Maaa okay. I just love. RaRa's okay. I love you."

"Yes, dear. I know, and I love you too. I promise we'll

hurry home so you can direct Willy and his men. How about some music?"

I nodded, "Yeaa, Maaa. Please." My happy attitude returned while Mom punched the black piano-like keys set into the dashboard. She pressed the second button and a light above the row of ebony dials flicked on. In a moment, the tune of "Happy Days Are Here Again" was piped into the rolling van that slowly advanced toward the city limits of Brookdale. My mood was brighter because rays of sun shone on the plate glass windows of the Econoline. I sat staring at the country terrain of silos and barns spaced out between fields of corn and soybeans. Occasional woods popped up from nowhere on my train-like ride through the countryside.

Chapter Seven

Mom wheeled me into the classroom, past the chalkboard, my desk and the dreaded isolation booth. She kept pushing me toward the center of the room, where Mrs. Lewis and my disabled friends had gathered around the "Show and Tell" table. We were always late for school, but Mrs. Lewis understood we had to travel quite a distance and always welcomed me whenever I arrived. I didn't care if I was late. Every day was the same and ran on schedule like a dairy herd that was milked at a certain hour regardless if the farmer wanted to or not. Mom parked me at the opening at the head of the polished table, while a girl with brown, braided hair was talking about her summer's adventures. Mom locked my brakes and stood behind my chair. "And I watched Bugs Bunny and ate pizza each day and that's all," said Christine. Her ponytail covered her silky white dress.

"How very nice, Christy." I was waving my hands at Mom, trying to shoo her away. I loved to be on my own. I experienced things differently when Daddy and Mom were gone. I guess I wanted to test my baby bird wings and see if I could fly.

"You go go. Now Ma. I okay, okay. But be here. Early because Willy. I got help. He needs me. To boss okay. You go. I love you." Mom hesitated to leave, but Mrs. Lewis gave her a reassuring nod and blinked her cocoa eyes at Mom.

"All right, Trey. I'm going. Have a good day. Bye."

She vanished through the maze of half-walls and quietly showed herself out.

Mrs. Lewis pointed to me, "What was your summer like, Trey?" She rested her chin on her left palm, waiting for the inevitable long reply that was coming. I took a deep gulp of air before divulging a detailed explanation.

"I good summer. Because bulldozer. And dirt. Because Cooter he is my. Neigh-bor had barn. Taken down. Because it old. Fire Depart-ment. Come burn. It down. Wants new one. For combine. And red truck. That dumps. Corn and beans. He combines. Daddy was at fire. I wasn't. Because Daddy busy help-ing. I sat. On porch by Ma. Barn go down. It took time. I sad because barn gone. But fun. Two engines. Were there and sky lit up." I paused for a moment to catch my breath before continuing. My classmates had stunned looks on their faces. Mrs. Lewis was in awe by my dialogue and large vocabulary. "After fire out. Cooter had guy. Come by bulldo-zer. And backhoe. And dump truck. Ma took me. I watch backhoe knock. Down stone found-ation. Next day. Bull-dozer push ashes. Rock in big pile. Load in trucks. I had ball. All day because knocking and shoving. Cooter let me come. And stay each day without Ma." I laughed gleefully at this last statement. "After gravel was spread. For slab. A road grader come. And smooth gravel all day. Cooter run over it . Four wheel drive Massey. He and I ride and pack. It down together. And concrete was poured. That awesome. Because of trucks." Mrs. Lewis cleared her throat and started to tap a felt tip pen on the tabletop lightly. "Cement cured. Carpenters come. Raised beams and rafters. With fork-lift. They nailed. Like watching. Circus tent go up. But wood and metal. Could tell more. If want but-" (Looking back now, my education was a slow evolution in the making. I didn't know it yet, but I would be about to break new ground, allowing me to leave behind a past of special-ed classes and start anew. It wasn't easy and took time, but now reminds me of building something piece by piece, like restoring an old car or house, to achieve a finished product.)

Before I went on, " That's enough, Trey. Thanks for sharing your insight. It was very informational, I must admit." My classmates were completely lost and said nothing. Mrs. Lewis stood up and headed over to me. "Well, I have decided to read a story every day, but Trey won't be with us, because he answers all of the group's questions," she said to the silent circle.

"Yea, but I like. Stories." She released my brakes and directed me to my desk. I was wondering what was going on, because in the past I always had to do what the others did.

"I want you to read by yourself while I read to the class." She guided me to my table and locked the wheelchair in place almost like anchoring a ship to a dock. Mrs. Lewis grabbed a textbook from a neat pile and opened the book to the poem "The Raven" by Edgar Allen Poe. "Call me when you need a page turned. I think you'll find it enjoyable but hard at first. If you don't understand a word in a sentence, look at other words around it and try to figure it out by yourself, okay?"

She waited for a response from me before leaving to attend to the group. "I don't know. I can. But I try." I sounded like The Little Engine That Could.

"Very good. I'm sure you can," she winked at me and returned to the hushed huddle. "Who wants to hear the story about the Three Little Pigs?"

An overweight boy with a belly that wobbled and golden locks waving on his head said, "Yes'um." His blue eyes reflected the sunshine, reminding me of Frosty the Snowman. Mrs. Lewis started to read the tale, but Darcy raised her right hand before she could finish the first paragraph of the story.

"Yes, Darcy. What do you want?"

"I have to go to the bathroom." Mrs. Lewis rose up a third time and carted her to the back of the room. I read on while the rest sat idly, but I was near the end of the page. Sounds of heaving and grunting echoed throughout the class for several minutes followed by an aroma of solid waste. The odor smelled like Limburger cheese or when Cooter was spreading hog manure on his fields.

"Okay, I ready. Ms. Wis okay." I shouted from the front for the page to be turned.

"I can't come this second. I have a mess here." She yelled at me from the rear and held a wad of toilet paper in her hand. "You'll just have to wait your turn like everyone else." She disappeared and went to work in the stinky water closet for a long time.

I sighed because I was bored and trapped between two worlds. I wanted to keep reading my story, but I was stuck waiting for a page to be flipped. I stared at the green slate above me and drooled onto the edge of my desktop. I watched the white foam bubbles pop from the pool of saliva. I flopped my hands over the puddles, pretending I was a short-order cook scrambling eggs while the clock ticked away. The truth is, I was being warehoused because there wasn't enough help for all of us and our potential was wasted. Beside the column of books was a chart that had five rows and the days of the week written at the beginning of each line. There were four columns intersecting the rows with headings of *Reading*, *Math*, *Spelling* and *Language* (which was reading comprehension). Our names were squiggled in red ink by each week. I read all of my assignments for the week and knew most of the work would take about three weeks to accomplish, because I always had delays in receiving assistance from Mrs. Lewis. I never had homework unless I was bad or impolite to a classmate. I didn't know what science or social studies were until I was fully mainstreamed. Mr.Gates, our principal, thought that was a waste of time since all we needed know was the three basic R's. (In later years, I always struggled in these courses because I lacked the necessary background to be successful, but I found a way.)

A bell rung for a fifteen minute break and I used my fist to hack at my brakes like I was hammering stakes. By pushing on my tip toes, I scooted myself over to the group, swung to face the window and gazed at the playing children outside. I sat there watching and felt like Rudolph the red-nosed reindeer not being allowed to play in any games.

Coming out of the restroom, Mrs. Lewis and Darcy had exhausted looks on their faces. I was in a stupor, glancing out and babbling to Kathy sitting in a wheelchair at a forty-five degree angle with brown cushions around her head. A harness held her midsection in a firm posture and a tan divider separated her legs. I felt sorry for her because she couldn't move an inch all day. "How, Kathy? I okay. What a day. I bored. Are you?" I focused my sight on her puppy-dog eyes blinking twice at me. "Yea, I hate here too. Was sum-mer okay?" I heard an excited moan emanating from her open mouth. I smiled at Kathy and propelled myself over to my motionless friend. I bent over Kathy to hug her in my long arms. "I wish you. Maybe talk. One day. I love you." I pressed my chest tightly against hers and squeezed all of my compassion into Kathy because I couldn't imagine what it would be like not to ever talk. I always will remember Kathy and have come to believe my acquired talents serve as a voice for the Kathys who can't communicate to the world.

The bell dinged again and I let go of her and moved backward toward my table. "Bye now." She winked at me. Mrs. Lewis helped the rest of the students to their seats, telling each what to do until she had time to teach us. "I go to Harris," I said to Mrs. Lewis, who was running around and putting everyone to work. I was back-peddling out the door because I always pushed myself to the Physical Therapy room where I would roll, crawl and kneel on all fours and look out the window at the east wing. I envisioned myself kneeling naked on the mat like I was admiring my erect penis in a mirror. I thought Miss Harris might be taking inventory of her equipment and supplies that she always did during the first week of school. I was doing what I always did. But today I was wrong.

"Not today. No Physical Therapy. I have someone to introduce you to. So go back to your desk please. And I'll be right over to get your spelling out." I went into the hallway and spun back into the class. I wheeled myself to the table where Mrs. Lewis was opening a book for me. She jockeyed me into position and locked the metal nubs of the wheelchair.

"Who is coming? I want know. Because I want. Now okay." I demanded in a high tone and slammed my right fist on the desk. (Sometimes I can be impatient.)

Mrs. Lewis had a strained look on her face. "Behave yourself this minute or you'll stew in the isolation booth for awhile." I was about to whine, but I bit my lower lip. I knew she meant business. I became calm almost instantly.

"Sorry okay. I be good. I prom-ise okay. What me do here?" I grinned at her to make up for my tirade and listened to her instructions.

She smiled at me with her hazel eyes. "I want you to go down the right hand column of words on the first page and try to say the word to yourself. Then you spell it out loud several times. Any questions before I leave?"

I was already sounding out the first word of the lesson while her wingtips squeaked over to Roy, writing away. His golden bangs kept getting in the path of his pencil. I wondered why women wore noisy shoes and always complained about their feet being swollen after standing in these tiny shoes all day. I pronounced the first word slowly. "Wed-nes-day. W-e-d-n-e-s-d-a-y." I spelled it out by myself and repeated the name of the day over again. "Wed-nes-day." I glanced at the book to check the sequence of letters and saw I had correctly spelled the word. "Yea, I got it. Right, Yea." I turned my head to the left looking at the pink curtain where the sick bed was for a place to concentrate.

"Un-v-er-se," I rattled off to myself. I peeked at the answer and felt I was cheating, but this was the only method of learning how to spell since I couldn't write on my own. I was disgusted that I had goofed. "I dumb because. I forgot i. You fool," I yelled. I stared determinedly at the word for about ten minutes. Some time passed, I shot a gaze at the curtain and gradually repeated the spelling "U-n-i-v-e-r-s-e." My eyes sneaked a look at the term again to be positive I had the sequence right, "U-n-i-v-e- r-s-e." I took another look and proudly said, "I smart I guess." I laughed and was about to go on, but an overweight lady trudged in, wearing a white blouse and a brown skirt and pushing a metal cart. She rolled in the contraption, which contained steaming mounds of food; each dish had a brown or green carton. The woman quietly delivered lunch by setting the plastic plates on the center table. She left in the same manner she had entered. My class used to go to the cafeteria but we ate alone, before the regular classes had lunch. I guess we were disgusting to watch eat. It was quite a challenge for Mrs. Lewis to haul, feed, clean and then take us back to our room. Now, I realize we were being segregated even more than when we were eating in the lunch room. We now had no contact with others and were trapped in our little world.

I was beginning to sound out the third word in the column when the bell rang for a second time. Clinking of crutches and the whispering of wheels from wheelchairs ran along the floor after the meal. I released my brakes and scurried over to the gathering like cows slowly ambling to a fresh bale of hay. Mrs. Lewis was opening up milk and sticking plastic straws in the tops. I positioned myself by Darcy and Kathy to make it easier to feed us since we were unable to. After making sure all the rest had the proper utensils, napkins and the bread was buttered, she took out my lunch from my navy knapsack and opened the tin box. I was having hungry pangs watching her empty out a sandwich, a bag of green grapes, a thermos and a flexible straw. She unwrapped my food and opened the jug to shove in the thin reed. She stuffed a towel in Kathy's, Darcy's and my shirts before any droppings stained our clothes. "I eat now. Okay."

Mrs. Lewis was spooning up some mashed potatoes for Kathy to chew before she gave Darcy a hunk of Salisbury steak. "And now it's your turn, Trey," I smiled and opened my large mouth before ripping off an end of the sandwich. "HEY, watch my fingers please." I almost bit off her right pinky, but I have accidentally bitten every person hand-feeding me food because of my gross movements. I giggled while she peered and studied the contents between the whole-wheat slices. "What's in here, Trey?"

Mrs. Lewis had a grimace on her face while she gave another spoonful to Kathy to eat after putting down the half of sandwich. When I had eaten my first mouthful and parcels of food were scattered on the dampened towel, I blurted out, "Liverwurst. And horse-rad-dish. And Mayo. You want bite?" I always liked spicy foods, because Mom made me try all kinds of dishes. Daddy loved hot things like salsa and horseradish. I always ate what he had no matter what was served. My classmates' soft, bland diets were normal for them because it went down smoothly and was easily digestible. (When I was in nursery school, a physical therapist taught Mom to feed me solid foods and told Mom I would gag a lot, but the reward was I would be able to eat anything, even raw vegetables. I will always be grateful that I can eat apples and steak, which are some of my favorite things. I wouldn't be able to enjoy them if Mom hadn't gotten me off baby food.) "It good." Mrs. Lewis shoveled a bite into Darcy, who waited for more meat. Mrs. Lewis then wiped her gravy covered lips with a napkin.

"No thanks, it's all yours." She popped my sandwich in for a second time. "Be careful of my finger, Trey." I yanked away and made the entire entity collapse in her hands. She put the remaining parts back together on a paper towel that was on the table in front of me. I coughed and she raised the thermos to my mouth. I grabbed a hold of the straw and chugged down a red liquid. I let go of the drink after a few seconds and took a deep breath. She brushed off the strands of spittle from me. Mrs. Lewis repeated the monotonous feeding ritual that was almost like playing three potato or a semblance of musical chairs.

Some time passed before there was a light tap on the door. Mrs. Lewis was finishing up and tidying Kathy's chin. "Come in please," she instructed the person in the hallway. I saw a slender black woman appear; she walked over to me while I munched on my grapes.

"I can come back," said the lady wearing a white dress loosely fitted on her thin ebony arms and legs. People always think I will be embarrassed, like I was naked or taking a leak, if they see me eating. I enjoy dining with individuals and don't care if I spill a little food on myself.

"No, it's okay. Have a seat. We're about through here anyway." The woman in the white dress and dark braided hair sat down by me. Mrs. Lewis tossed the last green ball into my mouth. "He is about ready. He just has a sip of cranapple to go." I was chewing away on the skin of the grape wondering who this lady was. I gazed at her bright wide smile and shifted a curious glance toward Mrs. Lewis holding my thermos as the straw danced in circles like an ice skater spinning out of control. I sucked the peel. "Trey, this is Miss Fredricks. Miss Fredricks, this is the character I told you about. Trey, you will be going to her class to learn grammar and history for two hours after lunch everyday. But you have to be on your best behavior and do what Miss Fredricks says."

"Um, okay I thirsty. Please." Mrs. Lewis brought the bottle up to my moist lips and I guzzled the rest until I was sucking air. I spat out the tip of the straw and she dried off the red droplets cascading down my jaw. I turned to the beautiful woman to introduce myself. "Hi, I Trey. How you? I okay." My eyes were gleaming at Miss Fredricks.

She smiled at me and said, "I've heard a lot about you." Mrs. Lewis was stashing the thermos inside the metal box. She pitched the straw and the sandwich wrapper into the garbage pail by her desk. "Why didn't you have any milk?" asked Miss Fredricks.

I belched and blew a blast of drool into the air. Most of it landed on the table but some dotted Miss Fredrick's skirt. I was amazed when her reaction was to swat the sprinkles by lightly stroking her left hand on the spots.

Some people would have been offended and just walked away. "I sorry, please. Forg-ive. Okay." I felt ashamed of myself and cast my eyes downward.

She beamed her pearly broad smile at me. "Don't worry about it. You didn't mean to. Now, answer my first question." I felt more at ease with Miss Fredricks because she treated me like Mrs. Lewis did.

I raised my head and leaned toward Miss Fredricks. I took a deep breath, "I hate milk. Because when baby. I always had juice. Ma was worry because. Babies always milk. But she give up. Because I stub-born. Somet-imes. I drink. Lem-ona-de, Cran-app-le, grape, apple. And or-ange juice and Coke. But Ma don't. Give me Coke meals. Because she boss. Only when go out. To eat. I can Coke. I eat ice cream each. Night with Daddy. He eats two bowls. I eat one. Ma always make sure. I have ice cream. Because of cal-cium. I like Maple-nut. Because Daddy says I nut. What your favo-rite?" I had worn myself out and sat motionless until the bell zinged again. When I was six months old I stopped drinking milk, and Mom almost went crazy finding ways to get milk down me by making puddings and custards. I didn't like milk, but I would eat ice cream and cheeses. Miss Fredricks stared at me while Mrs. Lewis dished up the last of Darcy's fruit cocktail to her.

Sounds of laughter and squeals from the swings echoed in the deadened classroom. Miss Fredricks shook off her awe by saying, "Chocolate is mine." I giggled and watched children jumping rope, performing double dutch for my entertainment. Miss Fredricks looked at her watch and announced to me, "It's time for us to go to class."

I was curious where I was being taken. "Where?" I asked, glancing up at Mrs. Lewis.

"To our class and it'll be fun. My students are looking forward to meeting you. I told them all about you." I was silent, thinking about what was happening to me. I didn't know whether to go or not, like a stray kitten leery of its new home.

I looked at Mrs. Lewis clearing the table of empty plates and milk cartons. "Hey, Miz -ewis. Is okay I go?"

Mrs. Lewis paused for a second. "Yes, Trey. Go with her." I was like a mental patient not wanting to leave the safe psych ward, fearing the unfamiliar world.

The wheelchair rocked back into the waiting hands of Miss Fredricks, who moved behind my chair without my knowledge. "Okay, I go."

"Glad to hear it, Trey. My class would be heart-broken if you decided not to come." Miss Fredricks pulled me backwards to get by the table and whisked forward for the door.

Mrs. Lewis said, "Remember to behave yourself." She trailed us out of the room, dragging the trash can and a chair filled with dirty dishes. She deposited them outside for the janitor to pick up. Miss Fredricks hung a right down the waxed corridor.

I squawked back to Mrs. Lewis, who watched my flight from the nest, even though I was bewildered at what was going on. "I always good." I took a sneak peek behind me and saw she had traversed her class. I slowly positioned myself in an upright posture while the wheels glided along the smooth floor past the kindergarten and first-grade rooms. I looked in all the open doors and wondered why

I was going to a regular class. But I loved seeing new places for myself and my eyes kept roving. The hall widened near the school's front glass doors, and rays of sun bounced off the tiles, making me feel special inside. Miss Fredricks turned left past the library that Mrs. Lewis's class was allowed into twice a year to see a puppet show. We could never take out any books. The stuffy odor of books made me sneeze. "Bless you, Trey."

"Thanks, I okay." I brushed my nose on my shirt sleeve and listened to the high-heeled shoes clinking behind me. They sounded like horses stomping on a wooden bridge. I reclined in my seat and glimpsed into the gym that had orange rims hanging down from the ceiling. I saw nets hovering underneath the hoops at either end and lines were painted on a shining wooden surface. In the center was a rack of balls that I thought looked like big navel oranges with black rings etched across. On the left of the hall was a series of doors labeled, *Storage*, *Boys locker room*, *Girls locker room* and *Janitor*. I snickered going past the girl's showers, because I kept envisioning water falling down firm breasts and soaking the hairy triangle between their legs. I became aroused thinking about the soft, damp female private parts and wondered why I always had an erection when I imagined seeing a vagina.

I jumped because I heard a clash of pots and pans in the distance. As we went by the cafeteria, I could still smell meat and gravy engulfing the surroundings. I continued to laugh when I saw the same lady who had brought the lunches to Mrs. Lewis's class wiping down tables. She dunked a rag in a pail of soapy water and glided the washcloth all over the tabletops like when Mom scrubbed the kitchen counter every evening. I saw a fat black man wearing blue overalls lifting plastic bags out of large gray barrels onto a flat cart. He hunched over the cans and tugged the sacks of garbage from the containers, throwing them on a dolly. It reminded me of Willy unloading bales of straw or hay from a wagon to an elevator and then stacking them in the loft. I always liked watching physical manual labor.

Chapter Eight

"Where go, Miss Fred-ricks?" My wheels rolled on, making a ticking noise as if a stick was caught in the spokes. I smelled a pungent odor of disinfectant issuing from the boys' and girls' restrooms. I was becoming scared since I had never been in this part of the school. "I go back. Because I don't. Belong here. I no. Reg-u-lar. I no good. I go back." But Miss Fredricks kept pushing me along between the vanilla cement block walls of the corridor that made me shiver.

"Sorry, Trey, but it's too late to turn back now. My class is due to arrive any minute. You'll try it for today and if you don't like being here, you can go back to the way it is in Mrs. Lewis's class. I think you'll like it here though. You have nothing to fear. No one will hurt or say anything bad about you, I promise." She aimed me into her classroom and I was puzzled to find no partitions in the open room. The desks were arranged in a circle and name tags were taped to the front of each student's personal space. Miss Fredricks guided me to an adjustable drafting board and my name was written on the easel in scarlet capital letters.

I grinned at Miss Fredricks. "I like it." I surveyed my new table and the lime sherbet walls that would become my learning environment for the rest of my elementary education. She sat, shuffling through a pile of papers, at her desk. Next to her grading book was a framed poem that read:

Teach Me

Teach Me
Please
All of your wisdom
So, I can became
A person with dreams
To pursue and be willing to
Take chances in life.
Teach me
To respect others and myself
As individuals by being different
And unique
We are all the same underneath
Teach Me
How to read, to write, to count and be creative
I want to learn from you
Show Me
I thirst for knowledge and guidance
Because I want to grow
I'm yours to mold and shape
Into the best person I can become
I'm ready if you are
Teach Me
PLEASE

(Miss Fredricks once told me a former student of hers had written the poem and became a poet. I admired how some people could put words together like a mason matching the texture and color of bricks to make a wall appear uniform even though each one was different in its own way.) I looked out the glass windows, staring at the children running, skipping, shouting and jumping on the black pavement between the sides of the red brick building. I was startled by a bell ringing and almost leaped out of my chair, but I wrangled myself in by tucking my arms behind me. I laughed, watching the kids race in and was amazed at how fast they disappeared from my view. I heard scuffling of feet in the hallway like a caterpillar was marching along a tree branch, looking for a spider's web to invade. The students began to trickle in and I checked out all the girls passing by me. My limbs tossed about because I was nervous. The pupils took to their seats in the circle. Some of the boys were whispering among themselves and a few of the girls avoided eye contact because strings of drool dribbled onto the floor. I felt Miss Fredricks touch my right shoulder and the room became quiet. I jerked my body all over the place until she gently calmed my tense muscles to a semi-relaxed state.

Miss Fredricks announced, "Class, I want you to meet your new classmate. His name is Trey and we'll have to be patient with Trey at times because of his speech. He is just like you and I except he is special like we talked about. Who wants to be Trey's assistant today?"

A silence was cast over the group for a few seconds, but a soft, meek voice spoke up. "I will Miss Fredricks."

"Good, April. Come over by Trey. Trey, would you introduce yourself and tell us something about yourself?" A slim blonde, toting a couple of books, rose from her desk and crossed the round space to a vacant chair next to me. I was frightened because I would be sitting close to a regular girl, but Miss Fredricks stroked my shoulder again. "You're among friends here. Just take your time and relax." I giggled when April sat down by me and my entire body was so rigid I could barely breath or talk. My sight was focused on April's breasts until my head jerked up to her freckled face.

I glanced at all the students who were waiting for a response from me. I laughed for a third time and looked to my left at April. I boldly said, "Hi, you cute. I like girls." The whole class roared in laughter at my remark. Even Miss Fredricks had to smile at my statement, while April blushed. I was proud about making the class happy and she settled down her students to listen to more of what I had to say. "I like outside. And every-thing. Okay I done."

"That was excellent Trey." I snorted. I was trying to control my giggling while Miss Fredricks, holding a red book in her right palm, stood in the center of the circle. "Class, please open your grammar book to page eight and read to page twenty about what is a noun. Then we'll discuss it in ten minutes. Get reading." I saw the class bow their heads as if in silent prayer. I heard a whisper that made me jump a mile high off my seat.

"Here you go, Trey. I'll flip pages for you. Just tell me when." I thought this was pretty awesome to have a beautiful girl waiting to turn pages for me.

I laughed again and said, "Yeah, okay." I turned my concentration to the reading. My head swayed back and forth. I was delighted at not having to wait for a page to be turned like I had to in Mrs. Lewis's class. I could read faster just by having a person sitting near and felt I was actually doing something. "Okay," I said to April intermittently, and kept reading slowly but steadily until

Miss Fredricks interrupted the quiet hush.

"Class, name two types of nouns for me?"

I saw a boy raise his hand. He had a crew cut and appeared to be a marine to me. "Abstract is one, Miss Fredricks."

"Right, Charlie." She nodded in approval at the skinny boy wearing ripped blue jeans and navy sneakers with white checks on both sides. "What is the other category of noun? Can anyone tell me?" An eerie silence inhabited the room until a sharp bang on metal shook the circle like a bolt of lightning had struck the class. My arms were flaying in constant motion and caught the attention of the group.

My mouth was contorted and drops of drool dripped down my lower lip. I struggled to pronounce the term, "Con-crete." It took a lot of guts for me to speak before strangers since I had seldom spoken to anyone but Mom, Daddy, Amber, Mrs. Lewis, Miss Harris, Tiny, Willy, Cooter and my disabled friends. In the years to come, my regular classmates would turn to me for the answers because I always remembered every fact and detail.

Miss Fredricks grinned and softly clapped her hands while I laughed. "Very good, Trey." The class was awed at how I was able to know the correct answer so quickly. All of them looked at one another in utter surprise. "Now class, a concrete noun is a physical object like a table or a sheet of paper. An abstract noun is a concept of something, such as an idea. I want you all to write examples of concrete and abstract nouns now before we go on to history. You've the next fifteen minutes to come up with your list." Miss Fredricks sat down at her polished wooden desk against the inner wall. I watched April tear two pages of loose leaf paper from her spiral blue notebook and I was wondering why she wrote my name on a sheet. She put her name on the other and printed *Concrete* on the left and moved over to the right, like a typist setting margins on a typewriter, to write *Abstract*. April drew a line down the center of each page. I thought she was making a reminder list like Daddy always did every morning, but why create two? I never forgot anything. What I didn't understand was that I was expected to dictate the assignment to April. I would soon catch on.

   April finished drawing the makeshift charts and began to jot down her nouns. I was glancing at a brunette busily writing away across from me. I was mesmerized by her brown eyes and hair. The angle of the sun striking her made her appear to be a goddess. My eyes tore off her clothes and I imagined the soft curves of the girl's body. My vision progressed downward to her tight fitting blue jeans. I felt sweaty and had another erection while I stared at her writing quietly. She caught my gaze and smiled at me. I was overjoyed in succeeding at get the pretty girl's attention. I laughed, causing all my new classmates to peek up from their work to investigate what was so funny. I tried to harness my giggling by taking a deep breath to relax, since Miss Fredricks was grimacing at me. Miss Fredricks said behind her desk, "All of you get back to work this minute or you'll serve detention." The class scurried back to their assignment while I bowed my head in shame for making trouble. I wondered what detention was because I had never heard of it. "Trey, get working or

I'll tell Mrs. Lewis. Don't forget our deal which is for you to behave like all of your classmates. Now start telling April your nouns." I slowly raised my face from a slumped position and glanced at Miss Fredricks's stern expression. She pointed to April whose pencil was poised and ready to write.

I blew a bubble of drool from my mouth and gave April a look of warning like a storm was brewing in the sky. I directed a steady gaze at April and rattled. "Okay conc-rete. Write gravel, water, sand. Okay cement, hoe, shovel, wheel-bar-row. Dust, tro-wel. And mort-ar-boar-."

"Trey, can you repeat the last word slowly please?" She smiled at me, making me concentrate on my speech.

"Okay I spell. M-o-t-r-b-r-o-d."

"Trey that isn't a word. Spell it again." I was getting frustrated because I wasn't a good speller since I dictated all the time to people like Daddy or Mrs. Lewis. I usually spelled out big words to everyone, including my family, but I would incorrectly spell the word. I couldn't picture the right sequence in my mind. If I saw the same word written in a book I would recognize it. When I was misunderstood by others and misspelled a word, I would substitute a simpler term for the first word.

"No idea okay," I had a twinkle in my eyes. "Okay ply-wood you. Dump conc-rete on. You miz it. You fill holes in. Tro-wel okay." April was dazed, listening to my description of how to prepare a batch of ready-mix like Daddy made to fill cracks in the basement walls. I always thought cement could repair anything, and when I heard concrete, I logically thought of the recipe for Sakcrete. I loved watching the fine, gray, dry powder turn into a huge mud pie. My new classmates had confused looks on their faces while Miss Fredricks signaled to April to move to the second list of nouns.

April shifted in her seat, trying to figure out what Miss Fredricks wanted her to do. "Let's go on to abstract nouns, Trey."

I had been gawking at the brunette's brown locks falling down her pale neck and cheeks. I almost fell out of my chair because I wasn't paying attention. "Okay, okay I will." I looked longingly at April and thought. "Oh I-I-I. Um I guess. I don't know. Sorry but I. Know make concrete. I will tell you. Again you get gravel. And-"

April interrupted me before I continued with my recipe of cement. "Trey, we'll just wait for history to start. I'll tell you my two lists if you want." She grinned and I nodded. "Well, for concrete, I had chair, desk, books, paper, pen and apples. And for abstract I had the President of the United States and holidays like Christmas and Easter. An idea or a thought are things a person can't see or hear but still sense." April paused reading, because I had become motionless and stared outside at the brickwork of the building. I felt stupid and empty inside because I was lacking the basic fundamentals I needed to be mainstreamed. I wanted to escape to my special-ed classroom where I knew everything. I would struggle in my courses for about two years, picking up the missing pieces and bits of education I needed to know in regular classes, like how to write a sentence or when to use past and present tense. By dictating, I never had to worry about tenses or making my sentences clear and concise.

"Class, please hand your lists in now. Your history

texts haven't arrived yet, but I have copied a handout for us to read." There was a moan of disappointment in the room and a rustling of papers being passed around the circle. Miss Fredricks picked up a stack of papers from her desk and gave a copy to each of us like she was dealing out cards. She put mine on my board and smiled at me while she made a sweep around the group. After handing out the two stapled sheets, she stood in the middle of the ring. "This is the Declaration of Independence, which our forefathers wrote." I thought Daddy had written the document because he was always writing notes on legal pads, and when I heard father I thought of Daddy. "Samuel Adams, Thomas Jefferson and Benjamin Franklin. We'll read the first two paragraphs now and discuss it. Your homework assignment is to read the rest tonight and be ready to talk about the remainder tomorrow." I was wondering why I had homework when I was being good. But I would learn that homework was a natural part of being in a regular class, and decided I would do homework because my regular classmates did. I wanted to be like them even though I didn't always enjoy being cooped up in the house doing homework. What kid does? "I'll read the opening and then I'll ask a question."

I sat silently, listening to Miss Fredricks's beautiful voice reading softly, like a catbird singing a tune in a tree. I almost fell asleep because I wasn't comprehending what was being said. She finished and asked us, "What do you think about the last sentence I read?" The brunette raised her left hand. Miss Fredricks saw her, "Yes, Carla."

My ears perked up because I was curious about what

Carla would say. "Everyone has a right to be free." That got me thinking about the question raised and I sat there taking it all in.

"Good, Carla." A black boy had his hand up. "Yes, Ned," she pointed her left pinkie at him.

"Each of us has an equal chance under the law no matter if you're black or white."

Miss Fredricks nodded. "Right." She looked around and saw April holding her hand up high like a star in the sky. "Yes, April." I was coming to my own conclusion.

"All of us can be independent and be what we want because-" I interrupted her because I had my idea and I had to get it out.

"Like I reg-u-lar. Class. I like here. Because I can. Be me okay." Miss Fredricks had tears in her eyes and grinned at me.

"Oh, Trey, yes," she said proudly. Neither the class nor I grasped the significance of what I said, but this was the first step in the right direction, leading me to higher peaks. Miss Fredricks glanced at her wristwatch, "Time to take Trey back to room ten. April, collect Trey's assignment and put it in his bag. Come right back here when you're through. And Trey, don't forget to do your homework." April reached over to grab the handout off my board and slipped the stapled pages in my knapsack. She stood up and went behind my wheelchair, waiting for me to unlock my brakes. I was pounding away at them even though I didn't want to leave. In the short time I was there, I had come to believe that I belonged in this classroom, but I was too young to know why.

"Okay I will. Bye." April started pushing me out the

door. I had a frown on my face. I bent my head before exiting, "I like here. Bye."

The class and Miss Fredricks turned their heads to me, "See ya tomorrow Trey. Bye." I was relieved to know that they wanted me back and I was liked. (Over the years, I would become just Trey to my regular classmates, and I would be treated like a normal person who happened to be in a wheelchair. But to the outside world I was a drooling, babbling freak without a mind.) April retraced the route Miss Fredricks had taken earlier. I was enjoying the ride, but the closer we came to Mrs. Lewis's room, the more depressed I felt. My disabled friends were already leaving for the buses. April and I had to wait to go in like motorists stopped for a passing train.

Mrs. Lewis and Kathy left the class last. I grinned at both of them, and Mrs. Lewis smiled at April and me, "Go right in. His desk is the first one." April wheeled me to my table after Kathy and Mrs. Lewis were gone.

April locked my brakes, "I'll pick you up tomorrow. Will you be all right alone?"

"Yea, I okay," I said assuredly, looking at her standing hesitantly by my table.

"I have to go now. See ya, Trey."

"Bye, Apr-" She warily went out, not sure whether she should go or not. I was looking at my spelling book in the dimly lit room and decided to begin sounding out the third term in the column. Facing the open door, I popped my head up and started to say the word when Mom and Mrs. Lewis entered the classroom. "Free-dom. Free-dom." I was smiling at them. "Hi, Ma. We go home. Because Willy chop okay. I help okay. I got home-work. In reg-u-lar class. I like reg-u-lar. I good. I pro-mise. Miz.-ewis." Mom and Mrs. Lewis were grinning over their experiment and pulled up chairs near me to sit down. I thought I was in trouble for flirting with Carla when I was supposed to be dictating to April.

"Happy to hear you like Miss Fredricks' class. I was wondering if you would do me a big favor by agreeing to stay after school with me for an hour each day working on your assignments for my class. I just don't have the time to spend with you during the day the way I should. And I'll be the one giving you Miss Fredricks' tests, because you'll be taking them orally. You can't take yours in the room when they take theirs. This means you'll have to stay here sometimes when your farmer friends are working in the fields. You'll be here doing homework. What do you say, Trey?" I thought long and hard for several minutes. I looked at Mom and she nodded her head yes.

"I will because. I like reg-u-lar. But I go to-day okay."

"Why, yes, you had quite a day." Mrs. Lewis, Mom and I sat there smiling at each other, lost in thought like we were admiring a beautiful sunrise. By being mainstreamed, I learned how to compromise, communicate and socialize with others. But I also taught my regular classmates and teachers that I was no different from them. I felt guilty about attending Miss Fredricks' class because I was given a privilege not afforded to my disabled friends who were trapped in that special-ed classroom. My family and I had to sacrifice for me to be a "regular" student. Amber came home to an empty house while Mom was driving me from school. Mom turned pages or wrote assignments I dictated to her and at the same time prepared supper. Daddy occasionally helped out when he came home. I wanted to give up at times because my basic skills were so far behind my regular classmates and it took me longer to complete my homework since I had to wait for Mom or Daddy to be my hands. Nothing would ever be easy in my life, but I would develop a burning determination to succeed. I gradually saw the odds would be heavily stacked against me. But I had made a promise to Daddy to become someone, forcing me to strive to be the best I could be.

Chapter Nine

    Daddy and I sat on the porch watching the wind ruffle the blue spruces, making them appear to be doing the twist. Corn husks flew all over. Willy was combining the field across the road. We watched the big red harvester eat and spew fragments of stalks swipe after swipe. At each end of the field was a red wagon waiting for Willy to dump his hopper of corn. I pretended the gravity beds were chamber pots that the combine peed its loads into to keep working. I always enjoyed the flurry of activity because tractors kept bringing empty beds, which bounced and banged like a kettle drum. In a short time each wagon would become a laden container with orangish yellow peaking out of the top.

    Mom came outside to fetch the mail and passed us, lazily drinking our lemonade and beer. My vision was glued to the farm equipment toiling to reap the crop quickly, because Willy had other fields to harvest. Daddy was chugging a Bud, thinking about something. I knew by how he eyed the bottle, holding it before him, examining the shape of the neck. I thought about the year Willy's elevator broke down and he was in the middle of combining. He had to wait for parts, but his crop was ready since winter was approaching. His hired men rounded up every available wagon, truck and semi-trailer from surrounding farms while Willy kept harvesting, filling anything in sight. The field was lined with overflowing vehicles loaded with golden grain. I thought this was neat, but it was a headache for Willy. It took him a few weeks to empty all eighty wagons and trucks. He had to return the borrowed vehicles to their respective owners.

"Hey, Trey." I shifted in my seat to face Daddy. "I was thinking about you and I going to Charlestown on Friday. I'm taking the day off from work and you don't have school because it's an in-service day, right?"

"Yea."

"Why don't we check out some electric wheelchairs?"

"No. I not bad guy." I thought Daddy meant execution chair because *electric* and *execution* sounded alike. I was afraid of being electrocuted because I knew electricity was dangerous. Daddy warned me to stay away from power lines and I had it in my head that anything electric was bad.

"Please, Buddy. Try it for me," he said urgently. He had been after me for some time about getting a motorized chair. All I imagined was the murderers on death row being shocked with electric current and I would die if I had a power wheelchair. It was one of those things a child's mind creates, like being scared of the dark, fearing that the boogy man might come. I finally gave into Daddy's wish because I always loved to make him happy.

"Okay, I will." He smiled and kissed me. He was overjoyed at getting me to agree to go.

"That's my Buddy." Daddy raised a mug of lime-colored lemonade to my face to toast his accomplishment. I latched onto the straw and gulped down my drink in one fluid motion. "Slow down or you'll choke." I drained the eight ounces of the tart juice and let go of the flexible

tube, sucking air. I couldn't breath for a few seconds because the rest of the lemonade was running down my wind pipe, blocking my airway. I was being a typical boy, gulping a drink to see how long it would take me to finish. Mom climbed up the porch steps, reading a letter. Daddy was taking another sip of beer. I noticed Mom's complexion was becoming redder with each word she read. I thought I was in trouble by how she turned beat red. "Damn them," she stomped her feet to arouse Daddy's attention.
"What?"
"Listen to this crap." I was curious about what had made Mom angry, but I was more interested in watching Willy work in the field.

Dear Mrs and Mr. Pike,

This is to inform you of a change in policy at the Aquatic Center. We have become aware of late that our pool is being used by nondevelopmentally disabled children. Since the Aquatic Center is a part of the Institution for the Mentally Retarded, the board of directors has elected to limit access to developmentally disabled children. To have your physically disabled child remain eligible for our services, he or she must be declared cognitively handicapped or be dropped from our swimming program.

Sincerely,
The Board of Directors

"Can't believe this, Sam." Mom crumpled up the wad of paper into a ball and threw it against the wall, where it crushed a spider web.

"They got us over a barrel. Damn't all." I didn't know what was going on because of all the big words. The Aquatic Center was a special natatorium equipped with changing tables in the locker rooms and roll in showers. The pool had ramps for wheelchairs to be pushed near the water, allowing a person to be easily lifted from his chair to the heated rectangle. The facility was built with the needs of the disabled in mind and the entire building was all on one floor, perfectly suited for less-mobile individuals like myself. Mom and I went every Tuesday night for a couple of hours, and it was a great way to relax the increasing tension in my muscles. I was losing my ability to walk in my walker because my hamstrings were bending my legs inwards.

"We have no choice but to withdraw our membership, Sam. If we don't, all of the hard work toward mainstreaming will go down the drain."

Daddy stared at her. "I agree. Trey's education is more important now. If he had that label of 'you know,' it would destroy any chances he might have in the future. That garbage would be on his record forever if we go along with them. He is so bright. I have a dream of our son going to college someday and being anything he wants." I was stunned by his frankness, because I never thought about even attending high school. I always knew I was different by how people treated me. They would buy me ice cream cones or give me a dollar at the fair because I was in a chair. In my mind, I was a regular kid. I kept hearing phrases such as, "Look at the retarded cripple. He can't even swallow. I'll give him some money because I pity him." (When strangers give you gifts for no reason except that you are a cute little boy stuck in a wheelchair, you only see the present, not the years to come.) "That's my dream too. Okay, we'll pull out of the program."

"Agreed. Honey, it feels like we take one step forward and two steps back. Every time we make progress the system fails us."

"I know. I have some sewing to do inside." She went in the house and we sat there, silently gazing at the reaper chewing the brittle brown cornstalks into shredded stubble. (Now, I can see that I was expected to be more than a person taking up space like my special-ed classmates whose parents demanded little. I was supposed to be a good student and always try my best even if I failed. As I became older I saw how the "System" that was supposedly designed to assist the handicapped reach their potential limited the number of options available. Experts told us that it would be a waste of time and money for me to attempt college because I was unemployable. I was on the honor roll in high school and had one of the best grade point averages. Imagine being eighteen, watching your friends go off to college and having to sit, staring at the television all day. My Mom would eventually put me through college and help me fight the "System's" rules. But even now all the accomplishments and the skills I have attained over the years don't mean much to anyone except my family and friends. Sometimes I feel like the farm equipment that Mike Fortson dumped in the woods because no one wanted to get their hands dirty and put it to use. I have to find my own way without any support or job because I don't fit into the "System's" game plan. It has made me want to succeed even more to prove disabled advocates wrong about their decision making. I don't know why I can't be given one chance to be a contributing member of society. Isn't that what America is all about?)

Chapter Ten

We made the trip to Charlestown as Daddy had planned on Friday. I was apprehensive but at the same time excited, because it was like shopping for a new pickup or tractor. We pulled into an empty parking lot beside a cocoa brick building with a plate glass showcase window in the front. Above the tinted glass were red medium-sized letters that read Byron's Medical Supplies and Service. I thought the store was deserted because there were only two white business vans parked near a loading dock leading to a garage door. We had taken the Econoline to see what size ramp was needed for my new wheelchair or if any adjustments had to be made to the fastening clamps. Daddy had brought a measuring tape, pens, index cards and a three-ringed binder containing his insurance coverage. After he gathered the necessary essentials, he unloaded me and we went inside.

Sparkling chrome gleamed in the sterile environment. Canes, crutches and walkers with plastic gray tips dangled from the ceiling. Manual chairs were lined against the picture window in all shapes and sizes. There was an open area near a counter where a man was writing. Beyond was a vertical line of hospital beds and to the left were toilets. I thought the steel triangle hanging down the hospital beds was a cymbal that Grandpa Jones played on *Hee Haw*. Further against the rear wall were the electric chairs and scooters. The place smelled like a combination of disinfectant and the interior of a brand new car.

The man looked at us. "How can I help you today?"

"We would like to check out a few of your power chairs to see if Trey can operate one."

"Oh, I see. Well, come over here with him and we'll see what we can do for him." He walked out from his counter to the electric wheelchair aisle and we followed him through the maze of specialized equipment. The gentleman yanked out a chair that had tiny wheels attached to a small seat perfect for Little Baby Bear to drive indoors on smooth surfaces. We knew we needed a heavy-duty chair with large tires for rolling over gravel, grass, snow, sticks and mud. Daddy shook his head, "Sir, we want a rugged wheelchair because we live on a farm."

Smiling, the man stood in his light blue shirt and darker blue dress pants. "Okay, but this is ideal for him because of his unstable balance." I was looking at the red print stitched above his shirt pocket that read *Stan*. He looked like an auto mechanic.

"I said no," Daddy used a firm tone. Stan was silent and had a befuddled expression on his face. (Most disabled advocates, including wheelchair vendors, have their own ideas about what seems right for me because of their intensive training. We were supposed to listen to Stan without any opinions of our own. Through the years, my parents and I have learned what will work and what won't by experimentation. We always have to go through these stupid big brother games because the experts think they have my best interest at heart. We are the ones who know my limitations and capabilities.) Daddy was eyeing a big brown Everest & Jennings, in the middle line of chairs, that had huge gray wheels in the middle of the line of chairs.

"We want to see that one," he pointed to the chair.

"Okay, but I recommen-"

"Yes, I know, but I want that E & J over there please."

"It's wrong for him."

"I don't care what you want. Now, please show us that chair, or I'll take my business elsewhere."

Stan was stunned by his bluntness and pushed the first wheelchair into its original position. "Why don't you two go back and I'll meet you in the front where we've more room to work."

"Fine." Daddy reversed my manual through the puzzle of medical supplies while Stan came from the other way. He was going forward toward us like we were square dancing. We converged in the open area, where I tried out the electric chair. Daddy transferred me from my manual to the power wheelchair and buckled me in. I was higher up than my old chair and felt I was going to fall because of being unaccustomed to the seating. I flopped my arms and legs all about because I needed to be fitted for a chair just like a suit has to be tailored properly for each person's body shape.

Stan had gone over to the counter to retrieve a legal pad, pen, measuring tape and a brochure about the model of the chair. Daddy was inspecting the steel frame. I had my eyes on the small joystick popping out of a gray control box attached to the left arm of the chair. He came over to us and looked at the manual chair, "I like how he was sitting in this one because he seemed upright."

"I agree. Why don't we keep the same seating arrangement?"

"Okay, by me. But your doctor will have to approve it, of course."

Daddy nodded to the salesman. Stan handed Daddy the booklet about the wheelchair and proceeded to take measurements of the other seat. I was bored to death. Stan was writing down numbers after each reading of the tape. He measured the width and length of the back and the bottom. Daddy was leafing through the packet and posing questions to Stan. "How many amps are in the battery?"

"Twenty-four."

"How often do the batteries need to be recharged?"

"Daily, and they have to be replaced every year or two." I sighed. I thought this was unnecessary since I wanted to fire up the chair and go. Stan was still jotting down information and looked directly at Daddy. "I believe we should keep the solid back and the three inch slanted seat cushion for him."

"Yes, we want that. Daddy was checking the width and the height of the wheelchair for the van.

"What color does he want? There is black, maroon, blue, olive, tan and vanilla." (I didn't know why some people always asked my parents what I wanted until I was older. I always know I am in trouble when a person refers to me as a pronoun and not by my name. I gradually learned to speak up for myself because I was tired of being overlooked by others. I'm an intelligent person capable of making decisions, but people treat me like a moron.)

"Blue, okay Daddy." Before Stan wrote down my request, he glanced at Daddy to see if he had understood my speech correctly. We knew he did by how his eyes rolled when I said blue, but waited for an answer from Daddy.

"You heard Trey. He wants blue." Stan quickly scribbled down the color like he was a waiter rechecking with Daddy to see if I can have a double decker ice cream cone or just one scoop. Stan walked over to the control box and knelt in front of me to explain how the chair worked. Daddy was on his haunches, and I intently listened.

"The wheelchair is driven by a joystick and goes in the direction you push it. For example, by pushing the stick forward the chair will go straight. It is the same for all the rest. The wheelchair has two speeds. Low and High. Low is the slow gear perfect for inside and tight corners. High is the fast gear and is great for the outdoors." My ears perked up when I heard that, because I always love to go fast and saw myself racing through the meadow after butterflies. "The switch for that is underneath the control station." I bent my head sideways and saw another box below. "The metal switch in the standing position means the chair is off. To turn it on, you flick the switch forward . High is backwards. Can he reach his hand to work the power gear?" He was looking at Daddy to tell me what he had said, but I already had my arm snaked around the joystick control by leaning over the side of the wheelchair. I raked my hand on the lever, making it fall back and forth several times before I took my arm out of the tight space by the gear box to regain my posture. Daddy grinned at me, and I felt like a race car driver waiting for the green flag to signal the start.

"Very good. Okay, now I'm going put it on low and

you go straight ahead over to the manuals." He was actually talking to me. (I always have to prove my understanding before anyone will open up to me.) I had one thing on my mind now, which was to take off. My fist grabbed the joystick and the chair whizzed to the other side of the room. I crashed into a couple of wheelchairs because I had clenched my hand snugly on the stick. I had difficulty letting go. "That's okay. Come back in reverse the way I showed you." I tugged the lever back like a slot machine and the wheelchair went in the opposite direction. I felt like I was driving a forklift with a crate and backing down an aisle of shelves.

I giggled when I passed Daddy and Stan because I was having fun. "Hi, Buddy." I said to Daddy, smiling from ear to ear, but I wasn't paying attention to my surroundings and bumped into a hospital bed.

"Look where you're going," Daddy warned, fidgeting with his glasses. I spun a clockwise circle around them tried my luck at negotiating the medical equipment. Periodically I thumped into a wheelchair or a piece of metal that clanged. But I made my way through the narrow path connecting the rectangle. I felt triumphant about my little adventure, because I was on my own. It gave me a sense of independence. I was riding in the open lobby pretending I was Mike, mowing his lawn, going in straight lines. Daddy was sitting at the desk and combing through a stack of yellow sheets. Stan was writing on a pile of strawberry colored pages near Daddy. I eavesdropped on their conversation when I made a pass. "How much will the wheelchair cost?" Stan looked up from his paperwork. "Oh, the basic chair without the customized seating runs about five thousand dollars. The special cushion and the solid back about another grand. I'll be the one making the seating." Daddy was dumbfounded at the outrageous price for a simple electric wheelchair. As I grew older, the cost of a motorized chair nearly tripled and still keeps rising.

I raced by again when Daddy asked a second question. "How long does a wheelchair last?"

"Five years is Medicare's standard." Daddy shook his head in disgust, thinking how many chairs I would need in my lifetime. Two every decade added up quickly. I took a break because I was having trouble keeping my hand on the joystick. It kept slipping off.

"Daddy make. It bigger." He had been studying my problem driving the chair and was already devising a solution in his mind. Stan noticed my difficulty too.

"Yes, I know Buddy. Maybe, I can cut off a screwdriver head and make it larger for you to grasp."

"I'll be happy to design a plastic one for you."

"No, thanks. I'll do it. I'm an engineer at Vip Inc. I solve problems on the assembly line and create molds for rubber parts that go in cars. Most of our business goes to General Motors. It was interesting, but I hate it now. Every day is the same," he sighed. "But I love inventing stuff for my Buddy. He is hard on wheelchairs because of his uncontrollable movements." Stan frowned, I think, because he was hoping to receive more money from us and our insurance company.

"Okay, I'll order the chair on Monday and it'll be here in six or eight weeks. I'll call you when it's ready." I was confused why we couldn't have this wheelchair in a few days because he had plenty of electric chairs to spare. I began to pout because I wanted to take the wheelchair home to show off to Amber and my classmates.

"I want now. Daddy," I said in a demanding yell.

"I know, Buddy. But we have to order first." He hugged me and put me back in my manual. I was crying, but Daddy wiped away the tears of disappointment. (The long process of ordering a wheelchair drags because of all the paperwork involved and the chair has to be approved by a doctor. Medicare or an insurance company needs proof of disability before awarding a wheelchair to a patient, and the doctor's signature shows a need does exist. The manufacturer keeps a limited supply available because of the relative short demand for their products, and can't support massive production like the automakers can. All of the parties needing to order a chair have their own time schedule. No one works in sync with each other, delaying the purchase of a wheelchair. Now it takes about six months to order a power chair. I have no choice but to wait for the mandatory Medicare's five year clause, even if my chair is outdated and no parts are available to fix it. I've listened to repairmen complain about attempting to repair the old one to keep me mobile for a few months. I can't imagine a person waiting to buy a new car when their old one has died, but the government tells them to be patient and wait their turn.)

Daddy gathered up his items and information. "Sorry for his behavior." Stan nodded knowingly at Daddy and exchanged the pink colored sheets for the yellow papers. They traded stacks like they were playing marbles or jacks with each other. I thought this was strange, but it was the wheels of bureaucracy being set in motion.

"I'll call you when it's in," he stood behind his countertop. Daddy shook his head and put all of the material in my knapsack. We went outside to the van, where the sun's rays gleamed off the tan exterior.

I was still brooding about not getting the electric wheelchair. Daddy unfolded the ramp and measured the iron grid's width. I was being quiet, feeling sorry for myself, watching the traffic flow along like sand in a hourglass. "Just perfect. I won't have to change a thing."

He loaded me into the van. I was silent but Daddy tickled me under my arms. I broke into a peal of laughter and became the smiling boy that Daddy loved. He was clamping the wheelchair into position when I said, "I can't wait Daddy. I go every-where. Without you. I can't wait. It awe-some."

He grinned, "I know, but we have to be patient, because it won't come for a long time." Daddy secured me and closed the sliding door. He went around to the driver's seat. I was gushing over my new power wheelchair and was already counting the days until its arrival. I had an annoying habit of knowing how many days it was until Christmas or Easter, and I would announce every day the number left to a specific holiday. He started the engine. "You can talk all you want about your new wheelchair today. Tell Mom, Amber and whoever else you want, but I don't want to hear one mention of it after today. Hear me, Trey." He grimaced in a stern manner, making a temporary impression on my mind.

We exited the vacant parking lot. I was stunned by

Daddy's high tone because he was always understanding to me. I remarked timidly, "Okay," to appease him as we disappeared into the steady stream of cars, buses and large trucks.

Chapter Eleven

The day had finally arrived for my first electric wheelchair to come. I hardly slept the night before because I was excited. Daddy went alone to Charlestown to iron out the small details like the insurance claim. He had to retool the joystick, and all of these things took time. Daddy stopped at Tilley's Implement Dealer to saw off the screwdriver and attach the head to the original joystick. He knew I would be revving to go when I first saw the electric chair. I felt like I did on Christmas Eve waiting to open my gifts, but we had to eat supper before opening presents, and that tortured me. I had to know what Santa had brought me right away.

I sat on the porch watching Mom stack firewood by the kitchen door. She traipsed back and forth from an enormous pile of seasoned logs, sitting near the garden. Amber was jumping rope behind me, singing like a blue jay at the silver blue sky, enjoying one of the last warm days before winter's raw cold. I was facing east, because Cooter was plowing the small segment of field that wrapped around the knoll. The open space was about twenty acres, and on the other end was a swamp that was too wet to farm. I watched the four-wheeled drive Massey Ferguson slowly pull a twelve bottom plow, turning up the brown soybean mesh littered on the ground into coal black topsoil. Cooter was roaring up and down the furrows to finish his plowing before the snows hit. I loved smelling the fresh earth being turned over mixed with diesel fumes, because it was like getting ready for a new beginning.

   I thought about how the hauling, skipping and plowing all required repetitive motion like the rhythmic pattern of a clock. I was thinking that time kept its own pace by either going fast or slow, depending on what I was doing. If I was riding a tractor, the hours flew by. But waiting for my new electric wheelchair seemed never to go fast enough. Being patient was the hardest for me to learn. I couldn't understand why anything labeled "Medical" had to be made, delivered and serviced. Sometimes we buy special devices to assist me in being independent only to find out them unusable for my needs. All of these devices, like a head pointer to turn pages, cost my parents an arm and a leg because we couldn't go to a place to try out a gadget before purchasing it. The head stick didn't help me, because the long metal pointer obstructed my line of vision, preventing me from reading. The head stick was shortly tossed in a closet to collect dust even though highly recommended by an advocate. Everything we bought had to be ordered from a catalogue and once used couldn't be refunded. From an early age, I was skeptical about technology. All the failed attempts at trying new apparatuses were disheartening and discouraging. I still had doubts about whether the power chair would operate for me while I watched the physical activities happening around me.

   I lowered my head because Licorice was walking up to me. I was about ready to grab his tail that was sticking up in the air as he cruised by. My whole body jerked when I heard the crunch of rolling tires rush up the driveway.

When I saw the van coming, I let out a shriek, making Licorice dart off the porch and into the garden. Amber dropped her rope and unlocked my brakes before I knew it. She was pushing me over to the plywood ramp that Daddy had built for the motorized chair. I was leaning almost completely out of the manual chair, but Amber somehow managed to get me down onto the stone lane. Daddy parked in front of the garage because there was more room to unload my brand new power wheelchair. Mom followed behind us. Amber struggled to steer through the loose pebbles. We reached the van when Daddy was guiding the chair out of the door.

"There she be, Buddy." He grinned like a captain before launching a new ship out to sea, and placed the wheelchair near the passenger door. Daddy engaged the clutches to allow me to drive the chair. Without doing this, the wheelchair doesn't move on its own. I was in awe, looking at the blue seating. The polished chrome caught beams from the sun, making the chair sparkle. The handle for the joystick appeared to be an Irish beer pub's tap, big enough for my grasp. "Ready, Buddy?" Daddy smiled at me. He was antsy to see me try to run the wheelchair and work his homemade stick.

"I go I guess." I was still gun shy about using something new and different. (It seems silly now, because having an electric chair lets me explore the world.) Daddy walked over to where I was and scooped me up in one swift swoop. I was in the wheelchair and strapped instantly. I thought I was an aviator getting accustomed to my new cockpit. I took a couple of minutes to become adjusted to the seating, because every seat feels unfamiliar after sitting in one chair everyday. Daddy, Mom and Amber were standing, waiting for the take off. I flicked the switch backwards because I had been thinking about how fast high gear was ever since we ordered the wheelchair. I rebalanced myself and with a strangling hold shoved the wooden handle into a forward position. The chair leapt, and before I could stop I had side-swiped Amber. She would be the first of many girls to be bumped accidentally (or on purpose) by my electric wheelchair.

I laughed, but my sister wasn't too pleased. Neither were Mom and Daddy. "Sorry, Yellow-hair."

"I'll forgive you this time," she said, suspiciously rubbing her right shin. I headed off before she finished her sentence. I firmly clenched the lever and traveled down a grassy drive toward the barn and the field. I felt I was on a magic carpet, because I was by myself, strolling along without anyone taking me where they thought I wanted to go. This was my first taste of freedom from others, and I was giddy. I went around a circle Daddy had created where we kept the gas tank near a white, corncrib shed. In the middle of the crib was enough room to back a wagon-load of picked corn. The unshelled ears were lobbed over the parallel paneling. But now only gophers used the building for shelter, or if Daddy wasn't through cutting the pasture, he left the mower there until he was finished.

I followed the curve past the peeling white concrete block milkhouse with the boarded up windows. I looked at the warped doors, stripped to the bare wood, making me sad inside. Once the dairy had been the hub of the farm. Beside the padlocked doors was a gray nozzle protruding out of the exterior wall for pumping milk to a tanker truck. Burdock and chickweed grew limply along the edge of the barn. I curled the last turn of the oval and parked next to a rusty spigot. This was my favorite spot of the entire farm. For as long I can remember, I would sit here for hours in my manual, watching Cooter and Willy harvest, spread manure, plow, harrow, plant and cultivate. It was the highest place on the farm, giving me a perch to see for miles and view many farmers working at different tasks at once. In the fall or spring, after I got home from school and had gone to the bathroom, Mom pushed me out to the old well to supervise the activity. She would come to check on me, but I'd shoo her away until Daddy came to tell me supper was ready, forcing me go inside. The barn's tin roof rattled when it was windy, and during dusk I imagined ghosts made the noises. Only Daddy could drag me away from the tractors and combines toiling in neighboring fields.

I had been gazing at the fresh black soil beckoning me to drive in the rich dirt. I drove the new wheelchair into the field because I wanted to be Cooter in his tractor. The chair went about a foot into the mix of topsoil and ground-up soybean plants before the rear wheels dug a hole I couldn't escape from. The notches in the back tires quickly filled with sediment like a mill wheel churning on a river. I tried to unjar myself by rocking the chair forward and backward like Daddy did one time after dumping some rocks in a wet area of the swamp. It worked for Daddy, but not for me because the wheelchair wasn't made to go tromping through rough terrain. Luckily, Daddy was watching me and came to pull me out of the mire. After he put me on the grass away from my first skid marks, he firmly said, "This is a wheelchair and not a pickup. Do not go in the field, hear me. Keep it in the backyard Trey."

"Okay, Daddy. I will." I was looking at the gently descending slope before me, wondering how fast I could go downhill. Daddy took me sledding in the winter and I loved having snow fly in my face. I gripped the joystick and raced down the hill toward a young tree at the bottom of the valley. I was laughing to myself because to any boy, going fast was always fun. I never before experienced the feeling of being able to choose where I wanted to go, and I loved having the wind blow my hair. I realized I had to turn uphill because I was in a little hollow, and I was near the field. I sat under the apple tree, deciding how to go up. I had three possible ways to take. I could ride up the same way I came, or I could use the easement along the knoll filled with ruts from Cooter's farm machinery. The other route was going up a steep rise. I choose to zigzag gradually up this embankment. Having an electric wheelchair meant making decisions I never dreamed of before, like sensing when the chair was about to tip over because of a steep grade.

I made my way up the incline carefully and slowly. The motorized wheelchair chugged along as the belts whizzed and grinded, straining mightily. I loved seeing a pair of tracks trailing behind me. I felt I was marking where I had been, like breaking twigs off bushes to find your path out of the woods. I had scaled the hill and was now in the side yard between the house and a grape arbor. I parked under a maple shedding its leaves on Daddy's workshop. Mom had gone back to piling logs when I heard the whine of the push mower. Daddy was trimming around trees in the front yard. Amber was chasing Licorice in the front, playing a game of some sort. The shrill screaming Amber made meant she was having a good time.

I watched the leaves dance about the open expanse by a light breeze, almost like cartoon characters performing a number for me. I was looking for something to do. I wanted to help out since I had an electric chair. Coming up the hill, I noticed knee high grass between the three rows of grapes. I thought I would run my chair down the aisle, driving through the tall weeds like Daddy mowed under the shrubs. I headed to the vines strung on wire, which was nailed to fence posts and spaced about five yards apart. The length of the arbor was about forty yards, and it was ten yards wide. I decided to charge vertically across the string of grapes rather than horizontally through the rows. That was how Daddy trimmed between the Elms beside the garden. The only problem was I didn't take into account the hidden steel cord. It caught me by the neck and flung my chair backwards. I was in a daze when Mom and Daddy rushed over to me. "Are you all right, honey?" Mom asked nervously. I had a thick gash underneath my Adams apple.

I was fine. I was laughing when Daddy flipped the wheelchair upright. I could tell he wasn't too pleased with me by how he stood frowning at my dare devil stunt. He walked around the chair, looking for something missing or broken before he spoke to me. "What in the hell were you thinking?"

I was quieted by his sternness and his reddened complexion because he appeared to be ready to explode.

He was rarely angry in front of Amber or me. "Answer me now. Dammit, Trey!"

"I mow like you. I sorry Daddy. Okay, I go now. Okay."

"No more for today. This isn't a lawnmower or a 4x4. It is an electric wheelchair. It wasn't made to be used like a bobcat. Your chair has limitations. Think before you do something stupid again!" He disengaged the clutches of the chair and headed for the front porch.

"No, I want go more. Please, okay."

"The matter is closed. Drop it. Now!" Mom walked behind us listening to our argument.

"Yeah, but I-"

Mom interrupted me, "I agree with your father. And the decision is final!" I didn't argue anymore because Mom had spoken. There was no point in fighting with her when she had made up her mind. I knew I had to respect Mother's wishes or I would be punished. We went inside the house, where Mom washed the cut and applied disinfectant to the abrasion. My neck stung for awhile, but I was all right and roaring to go on another adventure. (The first year or two I had the chair, I did some dumb stunts like backing into a clothes line pole, which cracked the battery, and getting stuck in muddy holes that burned my motors out. I would keep running the chair into the ground until someone came to rescue me. I gradually learned to be more careful, because if the wheelchair was broken, I would have to wait for parts to be ordered and the chair serviced, which took from a couple of days to a couple of weeks. I was made aware of the high costs of repairs by Mom, because she took care of the bills. We had to pay for the additional expenses ourselves since Medicare only paid for some repairs. I gave up my highjinks because I would lose my independence each time my chair was out of commission. My freedom became more important to me than pulling foolish pranks, and I hated being pushed around by others after discovering the pure joy of riding alone. I learned from my mistakes and to be responsible for my actions. I was growing up, turning into a young man.)

Chapter Twelve

Growing up on the farm, Saturday mornings were about running errands. I would play with my miniature tractors on the bed, waiting to hear the stomping of boots against the hardwood floors. Rays of sunshine bounced off the metal trucks and implements lined at the head of the bed like a farm auction was about to take place. I dragged a Ford tractor attached to an International grain drill, sowing my wheat or oats along the flannel sheets. The blankets had been kicked into a tangled pile at the edge of my bed. "Purr," I mimicked driving my RaRa down the imaginary field with my left hand tightly clasping one of the front wheels. My toy kept rolling while I tugged the axle forward, creating straight grooves on the soft cover by the planter. My arm would eventually jerk and shove the entire rig down to the polished wooden surface below. A loud sound reverberated throughout the house.

"Are you okay up there, Buddy?" Daddy shouted from below in a room being remodeled by my parents.

"Okay, Daddy. I okay. Get up please. Okay." I yelled back, waking Amber, buried underneath her stuffed animals, in the next bedroom. I always thought when my toys dropped, it seemed like cars careening down a steep mountainside and exploding.

"I'll be right up." A moment passed before I heard the clop on the stairs and along the narrow corridor leading to my room. The door cracked open and Daddy was smiling as he walked over to where I lay. "Good morning, Trey. Are you ready for your haircut today?" He lugged my thin frame up and onto his broad left shoulder.

"I okay. Daddy. You okay?" My belly was being jabbed by Daddy's steps, but the worst was going downstairs because of the springlike movement of his gait. "Hi, Yell-ow-hair." Amber trailed behind us in her pink nightgown as we descended the painted red steps, scratched from staples that once held a green carpet. She shook her head at me, almost saying it's too early to be teased by an obnoxious brother. Daddy carried me into a makeshift guest room, and Amber turned around the dark brown banister to where the big bathroom was hidden between the staircase and a utility room for the washer and dryer.

The smell of plaster and sheetrock dust hung in the air. Daddy negotiated our way through the building supplies scattered about. Hammers, a measuring tape and his pocketknife lay on a piece of plywood, covering two sawhorses, that was used for a cutting surface. We passed by a double bed that had my clothes already out on a torn, white mattress pad. "What doing? Daddy. I wonder-ing."

"Oh, nothing I guess, just spackeling the new wall and scraping out the gunk from the outlets." Daddy lowered me from his upper torso and contorted my rigid body into a standing position. I was facing forward now and saw a five gallon pail of Gold Bond sitting by a walnut drawer. The shinning blade of a putty knife was drawn across the lid of the can. My arms flung out in each direction when we approached the freshly spackeled damp edges of a doorframe to the little bathroom. "Arms in please. I don't want to redo my handiwork again." I pretended I was a pilot coming in for a landing.

Once I had pulled my spreading wings inward, Daddy proceeded to the toilet and set my feet on the new, cold vanilla tile, where the odor of glue was still evident. He slid my pajama bottoms to my knees and stood silently. I looked around the water closet, waiting for my morning erection to relax enough for me to pee. I noticed something strange on the sink and on the clean linoleum. Blue tablets had fallen everywhere. An open prescription container by the faucet was empty. I knew it was Daddy's high blood pressure pills and didn't give a second thought about the spilled medication. (I was on my farm where nothing bad happened or harm came to my family. Being an adult now, I would have seen the apparent warning sign of an overdose, but I was just a boy who believed his father could do no wrong.)

"My back has about had it, Trey. Hurry up and go. Dammit please." My penis was limp enough to allow me to do my business. He took me out to the bed and started to dress me. "Boy, I wish I could get that hard." I laughed at his remark while my legs were being tossed into my blue jeans.

"Why it get-ting. Hairy down there, Daddy?" I was talking about my testicles shooting out fuzz.

"You're growing up and becoming a man," he said, reaching for his knife on the sawing area a couple of feet away. I watched him stuff the sharp tool in his right hip pocket. Daddy came over to me to lift and transfer me to the manual, stashed next to the walk-in closet. We ate breakfast and I even had some toast because I was hungry.

Sucking a peppermint helped me keep down my food for an unexplainable reason. (Doctors don't know why it works. We always keep candy around wherever I go and I always have a piece after each meal.) While we ate, Daddy seemed withdrawn to me. I thought he had something on his mind.

I always enjoyed our Saturday outings alone together. We would go to the lumber company, hardware store, Tilley's or the gravel pit, picking up what we needed for the farm. I would go inside and survey the new tools, listening to men's conversations about the weather and debate how many boards to buy to finish a project. I loved being on the go, and Daddy wanted me to tag along because I was his Buddy. We sometimes went on wild goose chases. Daddy would purposely take a wrong turn down a back-country road to have the adventure of finding ourselves at the point we started. Normally I was the one directing him back to where he had veered off by remembering certain features or landmarks, like a color of a barn or a farmer working in a field. Abandoned farm machinery left to rust by the wind and the rain or decaying fencerows were other signs I used to determine our whereabouts. Daddy was amazed how I performed this mysterious skill with my photographic memory.

We headed west toward Brooks, where Daddy worked, driving on side roads, over the hilly terrain. I felt I was riding a roller coaster, being on a peak one minute and swallowed up in a ravine the next. I could see for miles on the crests of these hills, showing a few acres of woods scattered through the contoured fields. I was curious why the landscape changed drastically from flat to high ridges and valleys in a short distance. I poised my question to Daddy during a trip once. He told me a glacier had come from the north, depositing rocks and dirt to create a wavy outline of the region, but to the east the ice had stopped, leaving a level surface. I didn't understand his story about the mountains of frozen water moving down from Canada and giggled at his tale. I imagined glaciers only existed in the North Pole, and Santa's workshop was perched on a snow patch overlooking the world so he could see who was naughty or nice.

Daddy drove silently, and I gazed at the fields sparsely covered with dirty snow. Alfalfa meadows had a greenish brown hue until the arrival of spring. Crinkled leaves from oak, hickory, cherry and maple trees drifted like butterflies propelled by the stiff breezes across the open rolling fields. A bite was in the air that made my fingers go numb if I sat for too long outside, but the heater in the truck kept me warm.

We were about halfway to town, almost ready to hang a right at a fork in the road, when Daddy said, "I forgot something at the house. Godammit, I never have my head on straight anymore. Better go back and get it." His eyes had a cold, steely stare, and tears streamed down his reddened cheeks. I didn't think anything was wrong because he was always forgetting. I shrugged my shoulders, watching a farmer spread manure. I expected us to pull into a lane and turn around to return home. But he went left on a washed-out gravel drive beside a meandering creek that curved through pastures and tilled farmland.

(I had no idea how much trouble I was in for that

eventful morning as I rode by Daddy's side. I was always safe with him. He always caught me when I fell, or if I was sad he would tickle me to death. But in a few hours the man I idolized disappeared before my naive eyes and my life would be turned upside down forever.)

I thought we were taking one of our getting-lost journeys. I was happy about that because I hated having my hair cut. I was becoming a little uneasy about how he accelerated the pickup over the rutted track. I knew we should slow down before popping a gasket or breaking a shock.

"Nowhere, Trey. I'm so very sorry," his face was blank. "I have let you down along with your mother and sister." Daddy mumbled something under his breath like I do when I speak to a person who hasn't known me for long. I was bewildered at what was happening as we raced beside the rich fertile soil. Crows were scavenging the fields for kernels of corn on the snow covered ground. The truck bounced over gullies at a fast rate of speed, but came down hard when the wheels touched the stone surface. I dug my finger nails into the olive vinyl booster seat for dear life. I tried not to lose my balance and land underneath the driver's compartment.

I heard a bang from the bed. I glanced in the rear view mirror and saw my manual wheelchair had flown out of the pickup. But before I could tell Daddy about it, we were a great distance away from where the chair was deposited in a ditch. I was scared because this wasn't a game. He seemed unaware of his careless driving. We were in the middle of nowhere and no people were around to help me. I yelled "Daddddyyy stop now!" He was deaf and motionless. He looked dead ahead like a captain steering a ship on open seas. I had do to something quickly. A series of hairpin curves were approaching, and we would have gone off a steep embankment if I hadn't acted. With my right arm, I reached over to his bicep and wiggled my entire appendage around his. "HEY, DADDY. Peease stop talk. I beg you. Pleease, Buddy. I love you." He shifted his crying face toward me, nodding affirmatively. He cut the blazing gallop to a creep and pulled into a gravel pit. The Ford was idling while I wondered what to do. Daddy had to be ill. What was wrong with him? He was resting his head on the steering wheel, half asleep.

What could I do? I hoped a person would come by and help us. The quarry sat next to a pasture of Holsteins grazing on a round hay bale. I was trapped in the cab. I watched the spotted animals chew their cud. I was getting worried as time passed, wondering why Daddy wasn't moving. I had no choice but to sit and wait for a fisherman casting along an *S*-shaped creek that twisted through the grass valley and rolling hills. A narrow bridge crossed the road at the floor of the drainage basin before rising to a high summit where a farm sat. I knew a person could see us there and come to our aid if I waved my hands and signaled for help. But no one was about.

I sat looking at the fine material that had been crushed by an aggregate company and left for the county to use on dirt roads and highway shoulders. When stone was needed for repairs, the maintenance department would come with a payloader and their tiny orange trucks to haul it away. I was thinking what I should do. The only answer I could come up with was to scream for Mom like I did when I had a nightmare. Maybe if I yelled enough, I would wake up from the bad dream. All would be right and Daddy would be perfect again. "Maaaaa, Maaaaaaaaaaaaa, Help. Maaaaaaaaaaa. Maaaaaaaaaaaaaaaaaa. Help us. Maaaaaaaaaa." All the noise woke Daddy from his deep slumber and he smiled at me. "Is Daddy okay? Let go okay." He nodded before warming up the engine without saying a word. It was as if he were a toy soldier doing what he was told. "Okay, Daddy go. We go now." He went forward. I thought he would turn around to leave for home, but he drove behind the mountain of gravel. "No, Daddy. Go back go home." I was desperate because I knew we couldn't be seen by anyone if we stayed in the vacant space between the outcrop of limestone and the loose mound of rock.

"Sorry, Buddy. I just can't take it anymore." I was stunned by his bluntness. He always had something positive to say when I was down. I didn't want to believe the words coming out of his mouth. In my mind I was having a weird dream, and at any moment I would wake up with Daddy by my side, laughing over my imagination. He drove as far as he could into the pit until the truck reached a vertical barrier of stone. I felt like I was going into a cave or an underground tunnel because of how dark and damp the looming exterior walls were. Daddy veered to the right toward the mass of gravel and reversed the Ford straight against the jagged rocks, smashing in the tailgate. He paused for a moment, viewing the endless pile of pebbles in front of us. I wished I had wings to fly out of the cab and up to the sky to escape what I was to experience next.

My favorite television show was *The Dukes of Hazard*. I loved watching Bo and Luke leap over immovable objects in the *General Lee*. They would speed up an incline and fly through the air to get out of harm's path. Daddy seemed to be one of the Duke boys ready to ram up the deposit and go over the pile. I said to myself, he can't be considering what I'm thinking he is. It would be crazy. He charged the engine and plunged upwards on the gravel until the front tires sunk into the sediment. "Daddyyyy. Stop it. I scared go back. Go home to Mommy. Pleeeease, Daddddyyyy." We were about a quarter of the way up before he backed down and rushed into the wall again, busting the taillights. I was afraid of being damaged or abandoned like the shattered beer bottles dumped beside the outcrop, only to be discovered later by a work crew or a couple in love, hoping to use the quarry for a secret rendezvous.

He sped up and down the mound of pebbles, and each time the pickup scaled higher than the last run. I was so hoarse from all of the screaming that I vomited my meal everywhere. I slammed my head on the dashboard from one surge and became unconscious. I slid out of my seat to the space underneath the glove compartment. What happened after that point is anyone's guess. I was completely out for a period of time.

Chapter Thirteen

My body can't stay in one position for long because of the tightness in my muscles. When I sleep, I'm constantly squirming in bed due to the spastic nature of Cerebral Palsy. It is rare for me to be in a relaxed state without any motion from my limbs. I believe the soreness from being huddled in the confining area by the heater aroused me to become alert. I ached all over, especially my hams, being held firmly against the passenger door. Blood was trickling down my left hand that had been cut somehow and begun flopping in the chewed bits in my hair. I blinked my eyes upward and saw Daddy sitting there, waiting for me to wake up like from a nap. "Daddy help me. Boost please. I hurt and need. Get up now. Okay."

"Why sure Buddy. Be glad to." He grinned at me while he scooted over to me. Daddy put his hands under my armpits and lifted me up to my seat like he regularly did. We had an awkward time getting properly situated in the chair because of the lowness and the cockeyed angle. He picked me up from the floor, shifting the weight of my rigid body to the pea soup seat. We did it in stages. First, he put me on his lap and cuddled me. He had a guilty expression for what he had done. He knew he couldn't hide the attempted suicide from others. Daddy shuffled me across to my chair and tugged on the loops of my jeans to be sure I was centered correctly in an erect posture. He strapped the belt around my upper torso snugly in place by pulling the rawhide tighter than it was before. I don't know how the safety buckle came off. I probably accidentally hit the release button with my flinging fist.

I was surprised where we were because I was able to see out now. Believe it or not, the truck was parked in downtown Spring Rock on Main Street in front of a Barber Shop. *How did we get here when we should be in Brooks?* I wondered to myself. The blue, white and red cylinder was revolving a couple of yards away from us. I did a double take because I knew I had suffered a blow to the head. Maybe I imagined our joyride. But why did I feel lousy, and why was I covered in puke and blood? My mind said it was all a dream. Any second now, I would wake up and Daddy would be the same loving father I knew. The harsh reality was, both of us needed medical attention. My decision was to take control by demanding to get out or go see a doctor. He quietly sat behind the wheel, sobbing like a child who was being punished for hurting a sibling in a fight. "I really did it this time. I'm an utter failure. I let everyone down. Even you, my Buddy."

His face was turned toward me when he spoke these words. I was frightened and mad. I had enough and looked him straight in the eyes. "I want out here. Right now. Get out, Daddy. And get me out. We go in. Okay."

"Where do you want to go?" He stared ahead again and grasped the keys in the ignition to drive out of the parallel space because he thought I wanted to travel more. I sighed. What should I do now since we were on the move?

"No, no, Daddy. I get hair-cut. Because cool pict-ures. Mon-day." It was too late. The Ford roared down the main strip with the two-story red brick store fronts lining the thoroughfare. He zipped past the post office and the county courthouse with a greenish dome built above the clay exterior of the building. The ugly color of the cupola reminded me of Richard Scarey's book on how to build different structures. There was an exact replica of the county seat in my favorite story. (I always thought a contractor had seen the same picture and used the sketch for the design of Spring Rock's government offices.) I waved my arms at people walking briskly along the dirty walks, but Daddy cruised rapidly, blind to the outside world. A four way stop approached. I hoped he would have the common sense to wait our turn before going on. I was right about my fear. He barreled through the intersection without looking. Drivers honked at us.

I was angry now because of his total disregard for the welfare of others and me. We zoomed by the DiVall Funeral Home in the residential part of town. When I saw the white and green siding of the parlor, I knew action had to be taken now to save my life. But how was the question. I shouted at Daddy, pleading, "I had it. I want doc-tor. Because I hurt. Dadddddyyyyy lis-ten me. Please I sick. Hos-pit-al go okay." He kept driving past the neighborhood's two-story framed houses in various American styles found in every small Midwestern town. Daddy was deaf to what I said. I whacked Daddy hard on the shoulder by converting my arm into a stick to get his attention.

"Yes, what is it, Trey?"

I didn't know what to do or say. No matter what I did, he misinterpreted the meaning. I felt like an adult speaking to a child who was being stubborn, choosing to close its ears to the important words in the conversation. We neared the town limits past an A & W Rootbeer stand, an abandoned Kickapoo gas station and a cheese factory with a large gray mouse nibbling on a piece of Swiss. In my mind it was now or never. I had an eerie feeling of apprehension like a thunder head was about to burst over me without any protection. I was hesitant, "I don't want. To die. Daddy please stop. We talk?"

He was crying, but he heard me. He slowed his speed along the two lane highway. Daddy nodded. I hoped to convince him how much I needed help and wanted to end the madness. A mile or two later, he turned onto a gravel road because there was no place to rest between Spring Rock and here. We veered to the right where a muddy path ran through gentle prairies with grazing pastures, and dairy farms nestled in low lying valleys. I thought he would pull into one of the beautifully maintained dairies and red barns. I always felt safe at a farmer's house because of the relationships I had with Cooter and Willy. But Daddy went past the first and second milking operation before stopping beside a woods. On the left was a hayfield, and round decaying hay bales dotted the meadow where a baler had dumped the rolls of alfalfa.

He parked on a ridge overlooking boundless quiltworks of black, brown and white patches mixed between a few scattered stands of trees. I was nervous about what Daddy would do next. How strange it was to be afraid of a man I had cherished all my life. In a matter of a few hours, my admiration and love had turned to disgust. Going through my mind was, *What was Daddy planning to do now?* He sat there in cold silence. His left hand was in his left rear pocket searching for something. He glared at me, "I have failed everyone. Trey, don't become an engineer because I hate it. People are always telling you what to do and you can never finish a project before another comes. No, be something else. Anything but a fricking engineer."

"Okay, I will." I was confused why he said that, but I went along with what he wanted. Daddy pulled out his pocketknife and opened the blade by using his thumb as though he was going cut a wire. He spat on the angular sharp edge before wiping it off on his pants leg to clean the knife. I was anxious as to why he held the blade in front of him like a disc jockey speaking into a microphone. Why was he being crazy and careless, I pondered because Daddy was the kindest person I knew. It was so unlike his character to be destructive.

He broke the solitude by talking to me at a rapidly. His sight remained glued on the gleaming piece of metal. "Trey, you can be anything you want to be when you grow up. Whatever you choose to do with your life, always remember six things. Work hard and do every little detail of a task no matter how boring it is. Always be independent. People can take everything away from you but not your memories. Do your best in school. I'm proud to have a son like you because you never give up." He said the last two items very loudly. (They will ring in my ears forever.) "Make a dent in the world because I haven't. And always always remember that I love you." He drew the knife inwards toward his chest and stabbed himself repeatedly like he was carving a jack-o-lantern. I sat in shock, watching the blood stain his shirt and pour from him. I thought this can't be happening, but it was.

"Daddddyyy cut it. Out now please." He waited before turning the blade on me. "No, no. Oh please no. Daddy don't this. To me please." I felt a twisting pang inside me as he jabbed my torso. He stabbed my chest several times before giving my back six strikes. Each jolt increased the physical pain, but it was nothing compared to the emotional sadness I was experiencing. My heart broke into pieces. Daddy stopped his cutting on both of us and sat behind the wheel.

"I'm so sorry. Please forgive me, Buddy." I was in agony. I knew we had to get medical attention or we would bleed to death.

"Okay I will. Forgive you. I want doctor. Right now. Because I dying." I wasn't sure if he had heard me and was worried about what to tell him. I had to take a risk because my body was screaming for relief. "Okay, Daddy. I want you. Go back to farm. We get help now. Okay, Daddy." He started the truck again but went forward at a fast clip, weaving all over the road. "No, I said. Listen to me. Daaaddddyyyy."

My words went unheeded. I had no choice but to endure and hope to live. What a mess. Vomit, blood, sweat, tears and urine were strewn in the cab. I guess I took a leak in my pants when we climbed the gravel pile. Why was this happening to us? Was it my fault? All I wanted now was to hold Licorice, be with Amber while Mom fed me her homemade oatmeal cookies. I was too young for this. He kept zig-zagging on the lane for a couple hundred yards until the truck swerved off the road into a small ravine. We went up the embankment diagonally. One wheel quickly was thrust in the air. I held on tight and all of my muscles tensed up in a ball ready for the tumble. Daddy was in a daze and seemed not to know where he was.

In a flash, the pickup had rolled over a few times before landing upside down in the middle of the road. I felt like I was in a cage hanging by a thread, but I was alive. The windshield was shattered to bits and I was dizzy from the turnover. Daddy sat and stared into space, lost in another world, mumbling about the Galapagos Islands. I thought he was talking about Gilligan's Island. I was bawling my eyes out. "Daddyy help meee. Pleease I want. Doctor. I hurt and sick. All over please. Hos-pit-al okay."

His response to me was, "Yes, Trey, I hear you. We'll go to the hospital later. I want to tell you about the Venus Fly Trap which is a carnivore. We will go to Galapagos and then to the hospital. Okay, Buddy."

I was completely baffled by his lack of consideration for my well being. He acted like a movie star performing in a fantasy film in an enchanted land or forest. I had enough and yelled, "Help, help, help, help!" I was about to give up, but I heard a crunch of gravel behind us and a car door banged followed by a rush of steps. I shouted once again, "Heelppp pleease!"

A man appeared at my window, kneeled on the packed surface and peered into my door. "Are you guys all right? I'll go to a nearby farm and call for rescue." He waited for some kind of reaction to see if we were alert.

Daddy was waking up again and spoke to the gentleman. "Oh, no we're just hanging. Thanks for asking," grinning at the man who was surprised at how Daddy seemed to be unaware of our health or being in a wreck. It reminded me of sitting on the porch, sipping lemonade, watching a summer day pass.

"Go please help. Pleeease. I can't take. Any-more go, go, go. Pleeeasseee."

"Right away, son." He scurried back to his automobile and took off. I heard the heavenly sound of tires bouncing over the fine aggregate. I knew that help was coming and Mom would kiss all of my booboos away, making me all better. I was safe, I thought, but Daddy found his knife that had fallen somewhere near him. He stabbed himself in the heart, coughing up blood with each stroke. I decided to be utterly still and silent because I was afraid that he might attack me. Why did I have to witness this? It can't be true. Daddy quit and tucked the jackknife back into his jeans.

I was getting worried that no one was coming to our aid because we resembled mangled creatures from a horror show. Off in the distance, sirens were wailing, and I was relieved because both of us were about to pass out. My eyelids kept closing, but I managed to stay awake. Daddy was stirring when a paramedic jimmied open the driver's door. "Sir, where do you hurt?" The EMT took his pulse. I was about to fall asleep when I felt someone's arms unbuckle my seat belt.

The voice said, "Trey, hang in there. Everything will be all right. Don't fall asleep on me. Promise." A person picked up my entire chair with me still in the stool. How did this individual know I was disabled and needed my seat?

"Who here?" I could barely keep my wits. I wanted to curl up and go to bed.

"This is Cooter. Trey, where does it hurt?" Cooter placed me on a stretcher. My legs were bent in the shape of an arch. My hamstrings couldn't straighten out in a flat position like a normal person lying down. I saw his fire helmet on top of his head while he held my beaten body from falling over the gurney.

A medic was taking my blood pressure when I finally saw Cooter beside me and the sparkling red engine purring. Behind us was the ambulance. Emergency personel crawled in and out of its open doors to carry medical supplies to where Daddy was. "Get Ma okay. Because I want her. Okay okay okay."

"I promise I will when we get to the hospital." I heard the words *cardiac arrest*. A wave of medical staff hustled over to the pickup, but Cooter stayed by my side. He tried to distract me from what was occurring fifty yards away. "Hey Trey, I bet this is the first time you ever rode in a rescue squad."

"Yeah. Will you go me. Like com-bin-ing."

"Why, sure I will." I was scared because I kept hearing shouts "Stand Clear" and "D fib." I knew it was a heart attack. But I was too physically drained to become emotionally involved, and I was bewildered by the morning's events. I wanted to sleep for a long time.

"Coot get Ma. And Ico-rice. Because I want. Hug my cat. Okay." I always held Licorice in my lap when I needed to be comforted. I would pound on his sturdy frame when petting him and he had the patience to take the roughhousing from my gross movements. I guess Licorice was my security blanket because he always knew when I was lonely or needed a friend.

BUDDY WHY

"Cats aren't allowed in hospitals usually. Maybe an exception can be made in this case. I'll talk to the doctors about it and see what I can do." I was incoherent when the medic who had been working on Daddy came back, shaking his head no to Cooter. I half knew what the two men were communicating in silent gestures, but I was too exhausted to grieve. My mind was numb. I reclined on the stretcher and closed my eyes, but I still had a sense of what was going on. I felt being lifted up, rolled into the ambulance. I heard the sound of feet leaping into the steel compartment. I glanced out the doors at the truck, tipped over like one of my tractors lying on the floor after I pushed the toy off my bed.

I dumbfoundedly stared at the scattered pieces of glass around the wreckage and wondered why this had happened. Before the rear doors were slammed shut, I gazed out to the driver's side and said, "I love you, Buddy." I tossed myself back into my seat gradually falling asleep. Cooter held my right hand in his while sirens blared away.

Chapter Fourteen

I don't remember much about the rest of the day except having nightmares like Daddy and I eating silver dollars at a Burger King while others ate hamburgers. He kept feeding me coins, laughing when I threw up blood and broke my white buckteeth. People watched without intervening on my behalf. Another dream was riding on a conveyor belt at a Ready Mix plant, going up the elevator in Daddy's lap and following a trail of gravel and sand to the hopper. We were dumped into a gray batter and suffocated. When I woke up I felt like Rip Van Wrinkle because I was in a dark room that had a window. It was night because the street lights shone through the Venetian blinds. Where was I? I had tubes in my arms and one in my penis sucking urine to a dangling bag beside the bed. Tape was plastered to my mouth, holding a tube delivering air from a beeping machine with flickering red lights.

Out of the corner of my eye, I saw Mom slouching in a chair next to the door. She was napping, and loosely held a romance novel in her left hand. Tissues were crumbled up in a pile on a nightstand. I must have stirred my sheets or wriggled because Mom automatically rose up and came over to me. How did she know I was awake? Woman's intuition I guess. She brushed my bangs gently and spoke in a soothing voice. "Its all right Trey. Mom is here and I'll stay with you. I won't leave you, I promise. Amber is with Cooter and Licorice is well. Just go back to sleep because you need your rest." Mom pulled over the chair to sit by me while I dozed, dreaming about Daddy dying in a ditch or me driving the truck, unable to stop running through fields and over fences. I knew he was dead, but in my heart he was alive. Mom didn't mention Daddy at all. Why? The answer was clear, but I needed to hear the words.

I slept for two days because I had abrasions on my back and chest. I bruised my left lung from all the screaming I did. I had cuts on my head and hands. I felt like Amber's old Raggedy Ann doll that she played house with outside. I was well enough to be moved from the ICU to a private room when I was off the respirator. I learned how to use a urinal because Mom couldn't hold me up and I was losing my ability to stand straight. The physical scars were healing, but I was an emotionally confused young man. After being moved to my room, I was told by a psychologist that Daddy had killed himself. I didn't believe it because he was Superman in my eyes. He kept popping up in and out of my sight like a genie. One minute he appeared before me, being my Buddy, and the next he become his evil twin, wielding his pocketknife. I didn't know what was reality and what was fantasy. "Why he die?" I asked the doctor and Mom, who were sitting by my bedside.

"Trey, your dad committed suicide. He was mentally ill," said the psychologist, gazing sternly at me.

"What men-tal ill?" I glanced at Mom for an answer.

She cleared her throat and said, "He was sick in the head. He is dead, honey. And won't be coming back ever."

"I get it. I guess. Why?"

She dried her eyes with a Kleenex. "It's just how nature works."

"Oh, yeah like. Big oak. He and I cut. By woods. He said it sick. Because middle. Was hollow. Like choco-late dough-nut. He told me all. Things die over time. Is Daddy's time. To die?"

"Yes, it is."

"He go heaven, Ma?"

"Yes, he will."

"Good. I for-give him. He always my Buddy. Because he Daddy. I not mad because. He hurt me. Okay." The psychologist was listening to our conversation, trying to piece together clues of what happened because only I knew. Cooter and Mom knew something terrible had occurred because of the damage to the truck. Cooter and Willy kept finding broken glass, jumbled parts of the pickup strewn in odd places like abandoned farms and ditches. Things didn't add up for this to be just an accident. A mirror would be found in one location, and a taillight lay shattered in a different spot. It was a weird treasure hunt searching for missing pieces, and I held the important information to cement the entire mystery.

The psychologist was writing notes, and decided it was time to push me into what I knew. "Trey, tell us what happened on your ride with your father please. Start at the beginning and don't leave anything out. Do you remember?"

"Okay, I will. Sure you want. All of it?"

"All of it, Trey." Mom wept while I spilled the beans, revealing every gory detail of our trip. I felt guilty about making Mom cry. A heavy weight had been lifted from my shoulders by telling the dark secret. The lost links seemed to be coming together to create the picture of that morning. The psychologist winked at Mom. "You've one brave young man here. You should be proud of him."

"Yes, I am," she palmed my hand in hers, caressing my long fingers in her soft ivory hands.

"Well, the second step in the recovery is to tell Amber what happened. She needs to know. And Trey is going to do it tomorrow. Can you bring her to the hospital?" Mom nodded.

"I don't. I hurt. Am-ber and I love. Yellow-hair. No, no, okay okay."

"Sorry, Trey. Sometimes, a big brother has to do unpleasant things that hurts his siblings, but Amber will thank you later."

"I guess okay. I do it. I want Lic here. Okay, please. Okay."

"Fine, Trey. Bring Licorice too, Mrs. Pike." Mom shook her head while the psychologist left the room, giving me a thumb's up sign. Mom went home to tell friends and neighbors the crux of the tale. She didn't tell Amber. All she knew was an accident had happened and Daddy was dead. I hadn't seen Yellowhair since coming to the hospital because I was tired. I was always happy to be around Amber, because she had the magic touch of handling me by being a regular sister. We fought like cats and dogs, but if anyone hurt me in any way, she stood up for me. (I am still in awe by Amber's beauty and her bubbly personality. She makes me laugh with her rapid talking. When I teased her, she would always get even because it was a sister's duty. We have a typical brother and sister relationship.)

The next day arrived. Mom, Amber, Licorice and the psychologist gathered beside me. I felt I was the evil prince, because Amber had jumped on the bed carrying Licorice in her arms and had begun to tickle me. When I started to tell my story, her happiness changed to fear, disgust and hatred. Licorice was purring up a storm on my shoulder, making the painful act bearable. I could see I was hurting Amber more than Daddy stabbing me. Our young innocence was lost now because we had to grow up more quickly. I cried watching Mom and Amber bawl. I thought I had let them down in some way, and felt like dirty snow before April's rains came to wash away the blackened whiteness. Each of us cuddled Licorice, and he seemed to know we needed his love because he purred nonstop while we clung onto him for dear life. I was happy because he was the same furry animal I remembered before everything turned to utter chaos.

Chapter Fifteen

Change means trying or adapting to something new. Every small detail was changing for us since Daddy's death. Mom had to feed, dress, bathe and bathroom me now that Daddy had passed. She worked part time at Nancy's Fabric Shop in the notions department in Brookdale to make ends meet. Daddy was cremated and buried in a hilltop cemetery overlooking endless contoured fields. We still lived on the farm, but it was decided we would move in the summer to a subdivision in Brookdale. The farm was too big for Mom to handle by herself. Cooter plowed the driveway for us the rest of the winter. I was numb because I thought Daddy would show up one day like a magician pulling a rabbit from a top hat.

We converted the guest room to my room because it was easier for Mom than lugging me up and down the stairs twice a day. Mom worked on Saturdays at the fabric store, leaving Amber and me alone. She would get me up and dress me before going to work. I sat in the living room watching cartoons, while Mom was getting ready to go. She was running late. Daddy always told me two things about females. A woman is always late, and never buy clothes for a lady, especially underwear, because men had no sense of style or sizes.

Mom was all dolled up when she checked on me before taking off. "Anything you want before I go, like going pee again?"

"No, I okay. Go." I was watching the Road Runner race

past the Wile E. Coyote when a giant boulder landed on top of him.

"Amber is getting you a drink. Please don't fight with her and be good. Bye, honey." She lightly kissed my forehead and scrambled out the door in a mad dash. I was always amazed at how women can change their looks by putting on a dress or redoing their hair. Amber was still in her flannel, pink-flowered robe. She had a white plastic tumbler half-filled with Cranapple for me. She wasn't awake yet, and I didn't say a word to her.

"Here, you drink up." She shoved the straw in my mouth without waiting for me to open. I was sipping it down slowly, but Amber said surly, "Hurry up, fool. I want to take a bath." I was getting mad, but I complied by draining it in one swoop. I wanted her out of my sight until she was more human. "And don't you come in on me when I'm bathing like you did last week, pervert." She disappeared into the kitchen to take the cup back and returned through the den to the big bathroom.

I was wrong to barge in my manual to see my sister naked, but it was one of the demented things that brothers do to satisfy their curiosity. I was at the age when boys dream of seeing breasts and vaginas. I had discovered the physical pleasure of being a man. One night I was lying in bed imagining Carla was standing in her lingerie beside the dresser drawer, and she took off my blankets and pajamas. Carla slid off the rest of her clothing and lay close to me. I had an erection, and had my first wet dream. I dreamed I drove my penis into her spread legs. The sensation made me afraid at first because of the white sticky foam that came out of my genitals. I asked Mom about it, and she told me it was natural for males to experience. I felt embarrased going to Mom because she was a woman. I should have been talking to Daddy about this, like a girl sharing her first period with her mother.

I was angry and bitter toward Daddy for leaving me, because my role model was gone. I missed all of the activities, like going to town and talking about tractors, girls and tools. I was surrounded by females all the time now, and rather than going to the hardware store or the lumber yard, I was dragged along when Mom bought Amber new underwear. I would sit outside the women's intimate apparel department, blushing at lacy black or pink bras and panties on manikins. I wondered what I had done to deserve this torture.

Amber hid in her room because she needed her privacy from me. I was all alone until lunch, watching Looney Tunes. I'm sure she felt the same emotions of loneliness I did. Licorice took turns loping back and forth between Amber's room and the den, providing companionship for both of us. I would be sitting, bored out of my mind, and he would plop himself in front of the wheelchair and stared at me. "Hi, Lic. What's up?" He would lick his chops as if we were having a conversation. "Oh, really. How inter-esting. I okay." I asked him questions about girls and the weather. Licorice would sit there on a blue throw rug, purring at me until he decided it was time to see Amber. "Bye, Guy. I like diesel. See' ya. I love you. Guy." I called Licorice "Guy" because he took Daddy's role of being a male to chat with.

When I was extremely bored, I would play with myself by rubbing my hand on my crotch to escape the hours of being alone. After reaching an orgasm, I found I would fall asleep, leaving behind my despair and the anguish of the suicide for awhile. I would dream about a girl making love to me, or having a visit from the Daddy I remembered and not his evil twin. (I have always wondered what it would be like to have sex because I haven't ever had a physical relationship. Over the years I have had a few emotional friendships with women whom I can share my inner feelings and thoughts, but nothing sexual. I have less chances to see females now since I graduated from college. I miss talking and teasing or walking girls to class. I always had to be careful what I said to a girl, or I might be clobbered. I still want to have intercourse just once and give my love to a woman rather than masturbating myself.)

Amber scampered into the living room, waking me from my snooze, telling me lunch was served. She went behind the handlebars and pushed me through the narrow space past the TV, a sofa and recliner. We proceeded to the kitchen, traveling through the doorway and entering the brick room that had an odor of something being burnt. Amber rolled me over to the table and locked my brakes. I was seated where Daddy used to sit because Amber fed me on her right. I felt strange being in his spot; I was taking over and moving forward in my life.

Amber retrieved two plates of blackened pepperoni pizza from the stove and placed our food on the checkered blue and white tablecloth. "Hey, what does Dummy want to drink?"

"I no Dumb. Orange so-da. Yellow-hair." I was looking at the curled slices of meat glued into the cheese that had a tar-like appearance. The crust was brown and brittle throughout the rocky edge. I shook my head at Amber's cooking, because she would forget to check periodically on how the meal was progressing in the oven. She was more interested in playing her Motley Crew records and talking on the phone about boys to her girlfriends.

She took a can of Crush from the fridge and sunk a straw in after opening the tab. Amber strutted to her seat and sat down next to me. She jammed a wedge of cheesy hot dough into my mouth, making me jump because I'm sensitive about my food being too warm. "Don't spaz on me. Here. Drink this." I grabbed the end and sucked away at the refreshing coolness of the pop. "Don't take it all in one gulp." She yanked the straw before I could release it from my lips. Amber shoved another bite in. I was enjoying my pizza, chewing slowly. I wasn't anxious to return to the den. "Hurry up, Dodo. I have things to do. And don't gag on me because I'm not cleaning up your puke."

"Go hell Am." I was mad at being ragged on by her, because I was trying to be good, but I had enough of Amber's attitude. She glared at me and slammed a chunk of pepperoni in my mouth. Amber resented having to care for me. She wanted to be with her friends and go places on Saturdays the way she did when Daddy was alive.

"I hate babysitting you. Eat up because I'm sick of looking at your face." I ate quietly without responding to her or there would have been a fight. I felt guilty about being a burden, but Amber was frustrated. We all had to make sacrifices now that Daddy had died.

I finished lunch, and Amber brushed off bits of pizza

from my shirt, using a towel like an umpire sweeping home plate for the next batter. She whisked me back to the parallelogram-shaped living room and stationed me between the couch and the chair. Amber stood in front of me. "What channel do you want? And I'm only changing it once."

I was happy with the home improvement shows on the television because they reminded me of Daddy working on the house. "This okay. Candy. Hurry up."

"Don't throw up on the floor. I'll get a peppermint. Hold on." She dashed into the kitchen to get a mint for me to suck. She came bounding back into the den like a panther delivering its catch to her cubs. Amber popped the red and white swirl of candy into my mouth. "Is that all, your highness?" she asked in a smug tone while she held her arms akimbo and stood in a firm stance. She was ready to blow her top.

"Okay, go."

"Good riddance, Stupid." She vanished into the corridor and went upstairs to her own world, away from me. I didn't see Amber again until supper; I had four hours until Mom came home. Amber was being rebellious, but in my heart I knew she loved me. I loved her too. But we were just kids adapting to the new circumstances of our family.

I was alone now, watching men hang sheet rock or pour a cement drive. I pretended I was a foreman giving orders to my crew. (Some individuals think not being able to walk has to be a tragedy for a person. I was born handicapped and haven't wished to walk ever. Walking doesn't determine your mental capabilities. Some people act as though I must be dumb since I can't stand on my own feet. I accepted my disability because it's a part of who I am. I always thought of myself as Trey and nothing else.)

    The hardest challenge for me is loneliness. I became aware of what it felt like to be alone after Daddy's death. I would sit thinking of all the good times we had together. The older I become, the loneliness increases, because Amber and my friends have their own lives to lead. I rarely have any physical contact with people my age since graduating from college. I feel like a giant maple standing alone in the middle of a plowed field, watching the seasons change. Amber and my friends make me want to live, but I have thought about joining Daddy on occasions. Mom reminds me often of what hollowness suicide leaves inside a person. I have tried to be involved in society, offering to volunteer my talents to individuals who need writing help, but I'm told by others that my speech impediment limits my ability to speak clearly.

    Another reason I think about killing myself is that my achievements, like earning a degree in English, don't matter much to disabled advocates. They believe strongly in how the "System" works. I have seen its failures in my life and in other disabled people's lives. Advocates have always said that I should forget all of my opinions and put my trust in the "System." Going to college taught me to think for myself and see what others don't or choose not to see. Daddy was right about me using a computer, which has allowed me to become a writer. My computer uses voice recognition that my family had to pay for. The "System" believed I was unemployable, and that the computer program I wanted didn't work for a speech impaired person like myself. The reason why I became a writer was to change how the "System" runs, and now I know what Daddy told me about making a dent in the world. One of my dreams now is to earn a dollar to hang up beside my degree to feel I can be like everyone else.

I was worried about being sent to a nursing home after Daddy died because Kathy, my special-ed classmate, had become too much for her family to care for by themselves. Her father was an alcoholic and her mother bussed tables at The Last Stop Cafe at night. They had three other children to provide for, and Kathy needed around-the-clock attention. Kathy was placed in the Institution for the Disabled and was allowed a visit once month from her family. Her parents had to give up legal custody because they couldn't afford the services on their own. Kathy's family lived only a mile away from the home, but had to obey the rules of the institution. Mrs. Lewis told Mom and I about it after school one day, because Kathy would just stare longingly out the classroom window without trying to do any of her assignments. She had been a great student before all of this happened, but it was like her willingness to live had been zapped out of her. I took it upon myself to stride over to her during the first recess to give Kathy a bear hug and communicate in our special, nonverbal language. I was always amazed at how Kathy's eyes lit up like stars when I pushed myself over to her. She had tears forming when I left for my desk.

I lost contact with Kathy after I was fully mainstreamed, because it was decided I was smart enough to attend regular classes after the sixth grade. The last I heard of Kathy was that the institution had withdrawn her entirely from school because of the cost of transportation. In the opinion of the board of directors, Kathy's education was a waste of their financial resources and time. They used technical double talk not to appear to be the big evil brother. She had her own room and sat watching TV alone in the dark all day, seven days of week. I was lucky because Mom's strength kept our family intact, and she made a commitment to me. It wasn't easy at times, but I was able to become an adult who had many experiences Kathy never had.

    I learned how some individuals make promises they can't keep, only to renege on them in a short period. Mom knew that I needed a male companion to talk to about the unresolved issues I had involving Daddy's suicide and to take me places. She had arranged with a social worker to have a gentleman come to the house and do guy stuff. I was excited about this because I was craving a male to pal around with. One afternoon I waited for a man named Dale to show up at three. Time just slipped by without an appearance from him. He called the next day to apologize for not showing up, but he had had car trouble. I was disappointed, but I understood. He promised to spend a whole afternoon with me in the upcoming week. He came, but he brought his girlfriend and dog along. Dale was only at the house for an hour before he excused himself. He had tickets to a rock concert, and his girlfriend's favorite band was playing. He left, promising next time would be ours. I didn't like it, but I wanted to accommodate his needs. That was the last we heard of Dale. He never contacted us again. I was devastated. I kept wondering if

I did or said something wrong.

Over the years, I have made friends, only to see them drop out of sight for unknown reasons. I don't believe what anyone says because I want to protect myself from being hurt. I have an attitude of not having high hopes for anything. If a person keeps his word I am surprised, but if not, I just forget it. I won't ever get over losing close friends, because each one that goes takes a piece of my heart. Daddy was right. People can take away your possessions, but not your memories. In many ways, I live in the past, replaying fond moments like mowing the meadow in Daddy's lap or escorting my best friend, Sue, from her dorm to the library and talking about our classes. I know I'm loved, but I wish I could escape the unbearable feeling of loneliness. Living on memories isn't enough.

I had fallen asleep in my chair and woke when I heard the door crack open. Mom was standing on the threshold carrying a bucket of Kentucky Fried Chicken and a bag of side dishes in both hands. She shut the door. "I'll be right with you." Mom raced off to the kitchen to dump our supper on the dining table. She made a quick dash to the bathroom because she had to go and get the urinal. Mom rushed back to the den and unzipped my fly, crouching in front of me. "How are you, honey?"

"I okay." I took a long leak and was relieved because Mom was back. I didn't feel so alone. "I better. Now."

"Good." She disappeared into the hall, toting the half-filled container of urine to the toilet.

Chapter Sixteen

"Who will give me twenty for this silver tea kettle?" shouted the auctioneer, standing on a wooden platform. His assistant held the polished pot while a circle of people crowded around three hay wagons layered with housewares: blue china, silver bowls, pans, chairs, canning utensils, jigsaw puzzles, board games, hand tools and knickknacks. "I have twentyyy," he pointed to someone in front of him. "Do I have twentyyy-five? Twentyyy-fivve," he whined. A man raised his hand in the middle of the pack, hiding the physical identity of the bidder. "Do I have thrityyy?" A lady in a white dress waved a pastel sun hat on the outskirts of the human ring, near the garden. "Thrityyy," he barked out to the silent group. "Thrityyy going once, twice," he paused for a moment before ending the bidding. The auctioneer smiled and yelled, "Sold to the woman in the lovely white dress for thirty dollars." His helper picked up a glass punch bowl, and the auctioneer commenced the selling.

I was sitting in my electric wheelchair about a quarter of the way up the drive, looking at the road, lined on both sides with cars, pickups and trailers. A path wide enough for a vehicle was left open for traffic to pass through. The driveway and the easement were blocked off by a couple of Cooter's Masseys to prevent automobiles from tearing up the lawn. To the right of me were two rows of furniture and antiques. A camper was parked by the rose bushes where Daddy had put his truck. But a concession stand had taken over selling hot dogs, hamburgers, soda, popcorn and cotton candy.

Mom was walking between the two rows. glancing one more time at her pair of antique walnut chests with marble tops she had refinished herself. She went down to the end of the row to weep by the loom she used to make blankets and cloth. I felt sorry for her because she was giving up all of her prized possessions she planned on passing down to Amber some day. I was enjoying the hustle and bustle happening on the farm because I loved to watch people scurry about.

Cooter was walking toward me in his light blue, sleeveless shirt, faded jeans and a yellow Pioneer's cornseed hat. The front of his cap had a sprouting shoot of corn twisted into the shape of a soft pretzel, grimed up from the black earth because it was planting time. He came near me. "Trey, why don't you go in the backyard and keep people from dinking around with the farm equipment? We want the Ford and the Massey to purr when the auctioneer gets there. Yell at anyone monkeying around them because this is still your farm. And it will always be, even after it's sold. You grew up here. It will be a part of you wherever life may take you. You will always be a country boy at heart." (He was right about me not leaving the knoll. I can still vividly see the farm in my eyes, like a cherished place I escape to when I feel lost in a sea of loneliness or red tape.)

"Okay. I will." I shifted my glance because I wanted Cooter to comfort Mom. "Go over there. Talk okay." He nodded and jaunted through the thick green grass to where Mom was leaning against the side of her loom, crying. I spun around and grabbed the wooden joystick firmly, like a trucker putting the hammer down. The wheelchair zoomed over the gravel lane underneath the towering shadow of the two-story frame house. The middle garage door was open because a large woman was sitting in a folding chair behind a table with a calculator and a small gray box next to her. A piece of paper was taped to the entrance that read in red lettering, *Cashiers*. In front of the third door were three port-a-potties, reeking of industrial disinfectant making me want to gag as I passed them. I looked to the left since I was heading down the grassy path leading to the field and barn. I was sad, traveling along the single row of Daddy's workshop tools and implements. At the beginning of the line was his drill press, a wood sander, a metal grinder, a circular Craftsman saw and a trailer with warped wooden sides that had shovels, rakes, hoes and pitchforks. I continued onward past a Toro rotatiller, the push mower, the rusty disc, the three bottom plow, the grader, the Farmall front-end loader, the bushog, the Ford with the belly mower and the Massey Ferguson.

 I saw a couple of boys sitting on both tractors, pretending to be steering. I shooed them away. They called me names like "Drooling Goat" and "Fucking Retard." I didn't care. My job was to protect the farm equipment, and Daddy always said to do my best when I did a task. I parked by the water spigot, guarding the implements as if I were protecting my farm toys from the boogey man at night. I checked out anyone inspecting the equipment by darting over to the person and asking questions. Most of the time, I sat remembering riding on

Daddy's lap, mowing the meadow and how he whispered "I love you," into my ear. I realized Daddy's love for me was irreplaceable. It's funny how a tidbit from the past can bring a special recollection. I looked at the clay furrows crusted over, and the soil was cracking under pressure from the tender green sprouts of corn Cooter had planted. I was about ready to spring up from the muck and mire of all the changes in my life by growing into a young man.

I hadn't noticed, but the whine of the auctioneer was drawing nearer. I guess I had forgotten to patrol because I was dreaming of what once was. Only a small group of landscapers and farmers remained to bid on the tractors. Now I understood why Amber had hid in her room. Our homestead was being torn apart. I couldn't watch because it was too painful to see. I went around the huddle of men standing in front of the bushog and took off down the side of the lane. Cooter moved his Massey to let buyers move in vehicles to collect purchases that were too heavy, such as furniture, workshop tools, implements, firewood and the lumber in the barn.

I drove on the fringe of the driveway to keep away from the pickups and trailers trickling, in getting their wares. The wheelchair rocketed along the side of the house, heading toward the front where the empty hay wagons were. I kept going on, but wandered to the open area between the lane and the overgrown garden. I stopped the chair about twenty yards from the blue spruces that pointed to the heavenly sea sky with wispy white clouds floating above the trees. My eyes followed the tar streak and the steel bolts in the spruce that Daddy had mended by his own hands. Bark was forming on the two black stripes running up the pines and around the barely visible nuts. Why did nature have a way of healing its wounds, I wondered, but Daddy's emotional problems couldn't be cured like the spruces were? The Ford and the Massey with the bushog roared down the drive, kicking up rings of dust. The tractors vanished onto the paved road. I cried and gazed up again at the turquoise sky, asking, "Buddy, why? Why did you die? Oh, Buddy, why?"

I eventually learned that death and loss was a part of living. I had to keep on growing and pursue the goals that Mom and Daddy had laid out for me. It wasn't easy, because of all the barriers and predictions of doom made by disabled advocates, threatening to drown my future and hindering my chance of success. What disabled experts forget to measure is my heart and fierce determination to beat the odds stacked against me. I'm a ship lost on a stormy sea, hidden in the night, seeking a beam of light to lead me out of the darkness. I want others like me not to have the hardships I faced. The suicide made me mentally stronger to withstand the broken promises of the "System," but I don't know what will happen in the future. Will I be a writer advocating change, or quit? I probably will be as stubborn as crab grass that keeps popping up even after it's cut or dug. I will still be on the edge of the knoll, surveying the openness for new possibilities.

* * *

CPSIA information can be obtained at www.ICGtesting.com
Printed in the USA
LVOW08s1428210114

370324LV00001B/113/P